Love,

Mamma Grace

By

M. A. Cole

Love, Mamma Grace

ISBN: 979-8-218-41699-7

DEDICATION

Thank you for everything, "Forever and Always!"

TABLE OF CONTENTS

TABLE OF CONTENTS II

HELENE'S

In a world that often whispers, sometimes there is nothing else for us to do but listen. My most recent whispers, as faint as they may have been, led me to write this book, one that is more or less about another book, but so much more. Many successful authors stress the need for the first chapter to be alluring enough to catch the reader's attention. Then they say, create an interesting plot and then a twist. Both should be systematically interwoven throughout the pages. There are often challenges or specific character flaws that dance around throughout the first few chapters. But all that effort should lead to an ending that no one saw coming. A redemption of sorts. One that not only a book needs but also what the reader should feel. I'm sure all those literary recommendations are very important, I really am, but I've never truly considered any of those components. I simply write to honor those rare but definite whispers, and for those who taught me how to hear them.

For me, I've had many teachers. Most were family members, but there were quite a few friends who helped along the way too. Believe it or not, a little restaurant was often the main character in much of my story. The restaurant itself resembled a bygone era with checkerboard tablecloths and 50s music. That music was almost always boldly piped in from a row of chrome speakers evenly spaced across a glossy black dropped ceiling. It had those sparkly red bar stools. The ones that most kids and a few adults would spin all the way around, over and over again. There was also a vintage blue neon Motorola jukebox purposefully placed next to the front entrance. The most memorable adornment, however, was a six-foot, very life-like statue of Elvis Presley standing in the corner. For authenticity, it had a Gibson J-200 acoustic guitar proudly strapped across the king's right shoulder. That damn statue scared the hell out of me on more than one occasion when I'd sometimes have to open the restaurant way before daylight.

Regardless of my occasional fear of the king, I kept that statue there as a tribute to my grandmother. She absolutely loved Elvis' music. In fact, I'm sure she had a big hand in naming me Presley, but I often thought how I dodged a bullet with his first name. I read somewhere that more than half of all Americans have worked in some sort of restaurant setting at one time or another. Half would represent a big number, so I'm guessing there should at least be some agreement when I say there are days you just love the restaurant life, and some you simply hate. There were many times that I'd look at my work, and even my life in general as a self-chosen curse but if I was honest, it did bring just as many blessings, if not more. My grandfather started Helene's in the early 50s. He named it after my grandmother, and it was definitely an odd but unique mix of mostly Italian, and I guess you could say, country food. One day Helene's specials could consist of the most delightful Rigatoni anyone has ever tasted, and the next, some of the best pork barbecue that you could put in your mouth. But I'm telling you everything was always more than wonderful.

From what I was told, my grandfather's family was as poor as anyone's in their already poor hometown of Franklin, Virginia. Franklin did, however, have a few opportunities back then because it was also known as the moonshine capital of the world. I still laugh a little when I think about my grandfather's lifelong claims about never drinking a drop of alcohol. I laugh because I also knew the nickname that so many of his older hometown friends called out when they wanted to get his attention. Even more, I knew back then he was one of those who distilled and sold that ridiculously strong hooch to anyone who ever wanted some. From an early age, I realized if he needed to do something to take care of his family, he would do whatever it took. That's the kind of man he was, family first, regardless of the consequences, all of the time.

White Lightning, as he was nicknamed early on, brought his family out of that extreme poverty and eventually to Richmond, Virginia. He did that by selling so much of that illegal version of Mountain Dew. My grandfather was a huge man. He stood about six-foot-four and weighed every bit of three hundred pounds, but he was solid and ridiculously strong. His mere presence was intimidating to many, but once you got to know him everyone could see the kindness of his heart. I'm pretty sure the only thing that ever outmatched his size was that great big heart of his. I'm so grateful I got to inherit at least an ounce of that. His road to Richmond wasn't what you'd call a direct route though. He would have gone to jail for his backwoods antics if the judge in that small town didn't give him another option. I'm not sure any jail could have held that big man if he didn't want to be held, but as always, he did what he thought was the right thing to do.

The problem was World War Two had just begun and he'd be heading to Europe smack dab in the middle of all that carnage. I'm guessing someone had to sew two or more uniforms together for him to have any chance of having an appearance that came close to matching the others in his unit. There was no way he could have ever worn anything that was standard issue. Like with anyone who has ever been in a war, it changed him. It never changed his heart, or his love and care for his family, but it did make him more compassionate towards everyone. It wasn't a normal compassion either. It was a special gift earned from seeing so many atrocities in a terrible war. He, nor I later on, could come close to understanding how people could do such things to each other.

As his stories went, about six months before he was scheduled to return to the States, he got orders to Sicily. It was there near Palermo where that big ole country boy met who he called the most beautiful, sassy, and stubborn woman he'd ever known. We heard that loving description of my grandmother a million times throughout his life. My grandmother was not only his physical opposite, standing only about 5 feet tall, but she also had a much different disposition. Don't get me wrong, that lady was as loving and nurturing as him or anyone, probably the most so in my life, but she was an absolute fireball.

To prove my claims, I never heard my grandfather cuss, never, not even once, but I couldn't say the same about my grandmother with a straight face. When she got really mad, she'd even cuss at you in a different language. She is still the only person I've ever known who could chew you out. I mean rip you a good one, but for some crazy reason, you'd feel better afterward.

As you know, just like the restaurant, her name was Helene. From what I understand Helene means *"The light"* in Italian. That makes perfect sense to me because that fiery, sometimes foul-mouthed little woman was without question the light that always led our family's way. I loved that woman so much but, if possible, I think my grandfather loved her more. If there was ever anything he lacked, she'd fill by just being herself. I don't know how else to say it. Together, they made each other totally and wonderful whole.

Later in life, my grandfather would sit his grandkids down in their living room and tell us stories about his and my grandmother's past. Some of the stories may not have been as wholesome as what you should probably be telling kids, with all the moonshine running and possibilities of jail time, but all of us kids were always enthralled by his tales. I know we were even more grateful for being able to spend so much precious time with that gentle giant.

Speaking about jail, one of his most common reflections was about the second time he almost went to jail while in Italy. My grandmother's papers weren't cleared to go back to the U.S. with him. That fact presented a special problem for my grandfather. It was one that he was going to fight at all costs. According to him once he found the love of his life, there was no way he was ever going to let her out of his sight. Somehow, instead of heading to the brig for not reporting to leave as he was ordered, he got the military to allow him to stay in Italy until my grandmother and her young friend Grazia, Mamma Grace, as we later called her, could all go at the same time.

Mamma Grace was a family friend whose parents were killed in that terrible war. My grandmother's family, particularly my grandmother, although informal, adopted her when she was about ten years old. She was only eight years younger than my grandmother when they came to the States, and that big, beautiful man kept his promise to take care of both of them. Mamma Grace eventually moved back to Italy after she finished high school. I personally never met her until after I became an adult, but I always knew how special she was to my grandparents. My grandparents worked side by side for over forty years in that little restaurant. They barely left each other's side throughout that whole time. They worked what seemed like all the time, but they created quite a humble little dynasty together. More importantly, they produced a large family, both blood-related and many more not necessarily related by blood, but family just the same.

Some people say they grew up in a restaurant but when I say it, I really mean it. I was there almost all the time throughout my youth, and for me obviously later on too. Before my grandparents felt I could help but so much, I had this imaginary four-by-four prison cell. That was a true jail that I dared not leave for fear of being trampled by a family member. Helene's was always hopping too, but just like clockwork every effort was made to serve all to satisfaction. At one time or another, we had people from all walks of life come in. But no matter whether celebrity, mechanic, street walker, or anything in between almost everyone appeared to be on the same level once inside. It was almost as if those who entered had to mysteriously check their egos at the door before being allowed inside. Not quite everyone fully followed this subliminal rule, but most did, and it was truly a beautiful sight.

Once I got old enough to be able to help at the level my grandparents felt was sufficient, I didn't feel like the work would ever end. I was so grateful even at a young age to be around my family so much but a damn restaurant is a lot of work. I can still hear my often-excitable grandmother telling me, "Amore, get your *culo* moving," which basically meant hurry my ass up at whatever she told me to do. Almost always after being directed in such a way she'd then let out the cutest most supportive little giggle. For some strange reason, I'd always feel more motivated than before she cussed at me. I didn't think her tactics were very fair but after those times there was no way I wanted to do anything other than make her proud and hurry my ass up. My grandfather on the other hand was a little more direct with his requests. He'd often have a similar grin or chuckle after saying whatever he felt needed to be said but his words were a little more like orders. All I could think about saying after he barked out was, "Sir, yes sir," but of course, I never dared to. He was just as supportive and garnered the same if not better results, but he always vocalized his requests in a much more urgent way.

I loved the fact that my family was so direct about pretty much everything. There was never any talking behind anyone's back or hidden agendas. Feelings may have been slightly touched at times but there was always a smile, a cute little giggle, or a hearty chuckle that followed to make everything alright again. Besides, the perennial goal of the restaurant was to get the job done, and oh how that was accomplished each and every day. My parents were probably the smartest people in the family because although I knew my mother spent most of her youth at the restaurant as well, neither she nor my father chose to have anything to do with it after I was born. In a way it was kind of as if I was born to take her sentence. Both of my parents were young when they had me, and I guess they were out there trying to create a humble little dynasty of their own in other places. To be completely honest my grandparents, were, let's say quite overbearing at times so I ended up with them and at the restaurant more than anywhere else after a certain age.

I think that's how my mother wanted me to be raised so she gave my grandparents and that doggone restaurant certain allowances that directly guided so much of my life, whether I wanted them to or not. Looking back, I now realize how the time I spent there was so special. Even profits were secondary or even further down the line to what I'd eventually realize Helene's gave me. Places that are unquestionably built with that much love have a certain magical personality of their own. But life, as it does, sped by and soon wanting to follow more directly in the footsteps of my grandfather I joined the military myself. I never made it to Palermo, but I did make it to Italy just like he did many years ago. I was based in Aviano, Italy to be exact, and eventually made my way to a different war. There were more than a few comparisons to be made between my grandfather's early adulthood and mine but I'm not sure if I wasn't just trying to force things to be that way, or whether it really was predestined.

There were no cell phones or inexpensive landline calls back then. Heck, most people didn't even have a phone over there so I stayed in touch with my family by sending letters back and forth as much as I could. I missed my family, I did, but I was out trying to learn how to be an adult myself.

Unfortunately, in my case, I couldn't have had the same claims about alcohol as my grandfather did. As strange as it sounds, I felt the military gave me a freedom that I'm not sure I'd ever felt before. I didn't realize how delicate those feelings were though because the thing about freedom is, it can be falsely perceived and a stupid beeper excessively going off over and over again proved just how owned I was. The response to that beeper and the eight-hour flight that followed resulted in me being in a terrible war myself for almost two years. My grandfather was right again; war does change everyone.

MY ISA

One of the best and worst parts of my life that almost followed my grandfather's early path to a "T" was, just like him, before the war I found who I just knew was the love of my life in Italy as well. Her name was Isabella. Everyone except for me called her Bella but I called her Isa.

Truthfully in a way, I was trying to be a little different from everyone else but I mainly called her Isa because from what my limited recollection of my grandmother's Italian lessons were, Isa meant *"The One."* I don't know how I knew, but I just knew my Isa was the one for me from the start. It may not have happened near Palermo but just like my grandparents it still happened in Italy. As comparisons go, I thought Isa was the most beautiful, sassy, and stubborn woman I'd ever met myself. Again, the similarities to my grandfather's early life were just so uncanny. Isa wouldn't even talk to me at first, except to say, "No Americans, No Americans," all while shaking her head from left to right to let me know the seriousness of her objections.

I wouldn't give up though. I thought of myself as a big tough military guy so there could be no way this cute little saucy Italian chick was going to beat me. I think my persistence was so strong because from the start she reminded me so much of my grandmother, but in a more modern day, spicier sort of way. That beautiful pain in the butt didn't make it easy on me, but it didn't matter though. I could still tell she was eventually going to share those feelings too. She had the longest, flowing, jet-black hair and these piercing, extremely dark brown eyes. She looked like the most beautiful princess from a Disney movie but she was right there in real life. Her overly round deep dark eyes had these golden rings surrounding her pupils. It was as if those sparkling rings were there to signify, just to me, how special she would be in my life.

With my family being part Italian I could have a few *"discussiones"* with her after she finally let me, but I was far from being anywhere close to fluent in her native tongue. It took her a little while to let me in on the secret that she spoke English probably better than I. I guess eventually I said, or did something right because before long there weren't too many days that we didn't spend at least some time together. Most of that time, in the beginning, may have been considered as borderline stalking on my part because, like my family, her family owned a bodega. They also lived above the store in a little apartment. Basically, her bodega was a restaurant, a convenience store, and an apartment all in one. Every single day I'd jump on the J- train, which was the only train in the area that ran from near the base to a few blocks away from Isa's family's store. I'd always pretend like I needed something and in my mind that was the only place in the world that sold it.

I really didn't care what I bought. To me, it really didn't matter. Even though I was spending almost all my meager military pay on my daily trips to see her we were getting to know each other a little more each day. I really didn't know if her family actually liked me, or if they were just grateful for the extra daily sales but either way, after she'd ring me up for something I absolutely didn't need, her parents didn't mind if we went out on the patio and just talked for a while. I had to stay in sight of her father of course but that sweet, beautiful young woman had me mesmerized more and more with each visit.

My original time in the military, before the war was more like a regular nine-to-five job so that allowed for my much-anticipated daily trips to see my girl. I didn't miss a single day either. Eventually, we went to other places together throughout Aviano and the surrounding cities. After a while, I even had a standing invitation to her family's house for dinner. I think by then her parents knew what was happening. I completely realized how I felt about Isa on one of those trips to her family's house for dinner.

The way her family interacted with each other just felt so familiar and the way they treated me did too. Love is the most powerful of languages in any country no matter how the words come out. There was no question that in that language, she and I had finally become fluent. All the Italians I ever met seemed to be very traditional, so I made sure to ask Isa's parents for their blessing before I asked her to marry me. They knew I didn't have much money working where I did so they not only gave me their blessing, they also gave me Isa's grandmother's wedding ring to give to her. Things were working out so well that I almost felt guilty about being so blessed. I guess that was my biggest mistake because later that same day, the very day I got Isa's parents' blessing and her grandmother's ring my beeper started going off over and over again. Remember this was before cell phones and back then if the military wanted to send us urgent messages or call us back to base, they'd blow up our beepers until we reported in.

I knew she was on the J train heading back to us at the time. I also knew her parents and I were anxiously waiting for her arrival but I was just a young soldier and a little afraid of not reporting in to see what the emergency was. I can remember thinking maybe I could at least run into her at the train station because I had to catch that same train to get back to base, but that never happened. When I arrived on base everyone was running around frantically. I'd never seen so many people there at once. As my sergeant walked up and down the halls of the dorm there was no way for me to misunderstand what he was saying. We all had thirty minutes to pack, clear the dorms, and report to the hanger. I'll never forget it because my heart dropped as he kept yelling out "Boys we're going to war." A million thoughts went through my mind but regardless of what I had just heard all of my thoughts were still about Isa.

Originally, I thought I'd be able to return to her parent's house later that night, besides I still had her grandmother's ring in my right front pocket. It didn't take me long to realize that I had no way to contact Isa or her family. They didn't have a phone and even though I'd been to their bodega what seemed like hundreds of times over the past year I didn't know what her actual address was to later send a letter, if that would even be possible in a war. Either way within thirty minutes everyone was loaded in a C5 Galaxy headed to God only knew where at the time. There were no actual seats in those planes either, just rows and rows of cargo nets with hundreds of soldiers strapped in a manner that was a lot less safe than you would be on an amusement ride. I have to say holding on for my life was a priority during the flight but when we finally landed my confused reality landed with me.

LOST FOREVER

At the time I still wasn't exactly sure where we were because there were no trees or water in sight. There was just sand, the runway, and these old metal buildings all around. We ended up staying over in that hellish existence for twenty-two long and sometimes terrifying months. I had friends die and I saw firsthand what changed my grandfather. But even in my version of hell, there wasn't a day that I didn't think about my Isa. We did eventually have the opportunity to write and receive letters. I kept in contact with my family the best I could but I still had no way to contact that beautiful little Italian woman. I often wondered and even prayed that somehow, she could find a way to understand what happened and why I had to leave in the way that I did, but the truth is I guess I'll never know.

After the first six months, the actual fighting part of the war calmed down quite a bit. As selfish as it sounds, I didn't know whether I was happy about that or not because that's when the real war in my mind began. Don't get me wrong I didn't want to be a part of any more bloodshed but at least during those times, my mind wasn't killing me. On many of those less active days, I'd try and find somewhere to be alone, whether it was behind a sand dune or in my tent if no one else was there. I'd just close my eyes with Isa's grandmother's ring in my hand and I'd imagine what our wedding day would have been like. Then I'd see our kids playing. I even saw us in our golden years walking together hand in hand on a sandy beach.

I don't know why I did that to myself, it never made things easier but while I was imagining what could have been I somehow sent myself to a world that was as peaceful and real as it could be. It didn't take long for me to realize that I wasn't afraid of dying, I was afraid of not living, especially a life without that girl.

I think it was some kind of subliminal self-protectionary method because a numbness came over me towards the last few months there. That was a feeling I'd never felt before. I'm guessing my heart was so roughed up for so many reasons that it had to protect itself and it wasn't so sure I'd do it myself.

We did, well most of us did, eventually make it back to our base in Aviano. I don't think I fully realized what I lost until after we processed back on the base after the war. Once processed we were allowed to leave. I already knew where I was going. I had no idea what I was going to say but I still knew. There was no question I was going to see Isa as fast as I could. I still loved her as much as I ever did but I also had to ask myself how she could still have the same feelings after I left the way I did. I basically stole her grandmother's ring and disappeared for almost two years with no word about where I was or what I had been doing. How could she ever forgive me? I thought. I could tell from my heart beating out of my chest that the numbness I once had finally disappeared.

As I was getting off the J-train I said the most profound prayer of my life. I asked for forgiveness and understanding. I also asked for the words that I was getting ready to say to that beautiful Italian girl to be from the highest intelligence and not just from me. I figured if my words came from a love even greater than mine then maybe I'd at least have a chance. Regardless of how sincere or reflective I was when I got to the bodega, I fully realized all the words I just so wholeheartedly spouted out resulted in nothing more than another unanswered prayer. It was now Isa's turn to disappear and that damn numbness set in once again. The bodega, the same quaint little place where Isa and her family once worked and lived, and the same one where I met the love of my life was all boarded up and appeared it had been that way for quite a while.

I frantically went around and asked all the neighboring businesses if anyone knew where Isa and her family went but no one knew. I then jumped over the cast iron fence that surrounded the bodega's patio and sat at one of the tables where Isa and I had so many of our original talks. This time, once again it was just me, by myself, sitting there with Isa's grandmother's ring in my hand. My life over the past few years was almost ridiculous but after that day I strayed pretty far away from my grandfather's past claims about alcohol. For the next few months, alcohol seemed to be my only chance at relief.

I knew a drink never really fixed anything. It just hides your feelings for a while only to ignite those same feelings for a harsher reunion at a later time, but I didn't care. When your soul is starving so badly sometimes all you can do is feed it with what you have. All of that drinking and sometimes fighting got so bad in such a short amount of time I thought I might be going to jail myself. I guess irony was striking again because I, like my grandfather did so many years ago, ended up in front of a judge of sorts giving me other options as well.

I was already in the military so that obviously wasn't it, but another base was. My master sergeant, the one who gave me the options, wasn't a politician or a non-caring high-ranking officer, he was a real leader and he understood. He knew what I and the others who had just returned from the war were going through. We each had our own stories but almost all of them had some sort of a jagged edge attached to them. He and his decisions proved to all of us that he didn't want us to throw our lives away before they really began. He felt we all needed a fair chance to figure out how to put our lives back together after the war. So personally, my choices were to re-enlist and accept new orders to Japan, or since my enlistment was almost over to take an honorable discharge, a couple of fake medals for my service, and hang up my boots and stripes forever.

I didn't have a clue what I was going to do. Ever since I was more or less lost in a bottle for the past few months I hadn't spoken or written to my family. Once I did, however, I realized how frantically worried they were about me. In a way, they made my decision for me and I'd be heading home once again. It was always my plan for me and Isa to make a life out of the military, but Isa wasn't there anymore and what I used to know about myself wasn't either. Speaking with my family left me feeling like a child who desperately needed them. I'll never know how my life would have turned out if I had stayed in the military, but I did know I'd never regret going back home to those who loved me the most.

MAMMA GRACE

When I got back home, I sulked around for almost a month but just like when my beeper kept going off to go to war, I had another important request that put me on another demanded mission. Just like the last, that was an order that I couldn't refuse even if I wanted to. It was my grandfather and he once again said he needed help at the restaurant. I can't say I didn't see that visit eventually coming. I can't even say that I didn't want it to come, but I don't care if I was sad, mad, or indifferent there was no way my grandfather would ever let me refuse one of his requests nor ever a day I'd want to. Back in Italy Isa and I did call my family together a few times from a base phone. She did get to speak with my parents and grandparents. They at least heard her voice and some of our stories.

I think my grandmother really liked Isa and could see some of the comparisons between Isa and herself. I'm sure she had some plans of her own for us, but she never got the chance. When my grandfather and I arrived at the restaurant the next day, I was lagging behind, but it didn't matter because my grandmother had something else in mind for me that day. She walked out of the restaurant as soon as my grandfather walked in. It was almost as if they were professional wrestlers perfectly timing the tag in. Just like old times, my grandmother grabbed my right arm and told me to sit my *culo* down. We sat down on our version of a patio, the curb. She then pulled out a letter that someone wrote to her. It was from Isa.

Evidentially some time before my disappearance, Isa wrote to my grandmother telling her about our Italian adventures and more or less thanking my family for how they raised me. She ended her letter with an acknowledgment of how much she loved me and even though she never met any of my family members, she wrote about her love towards them as well. My grandmother knew how much I was hurting, and she did everything she could to ease the pain, not only from Isa but also from the aftermath of the war. Even my greatest fan couldn't come close to soothing my broken heart that day. I was there to start helping but that first day I never went inside.

This bonehead who once thought he was such a tough military guy just sat there crying like a baby on my grandmother's shoulder. I wasn't sure if I'd ever feel life was fair again. I still don't know what I could have done differently but I do know I never felt that I did enough. I did write back to the return address on Isa's letters after I saw it that day. Even though it was years later I must have written a hundred letters or more trying to plead my case about what happened, but it was no use, I never got a response. I wished that Isa had written to my grandmother again as well but that never happened either. A million what-ifs flowed through my mind but again not even one ever created the solution I prayed for.

Finally, I just had to conclude that I couldn't spend every day blubbering on my grandmother's shoulder or feeling sorry for what could have been any longer. I eventually pulled all I could together and actually started working at Helene's, just like everyone always expected me to do. At that point, I'd been away from home for a little over four years and even though I was supposedly in the prime of my life I could tell my grandparents had aged quite a bit since I'd been gone. I soon learned they were planning to retire sometime during the year, but the specifics weren't quite worked out at the time. My grandparents had been running that restaurant for so many years, of course with ample help but I couldn't envision a Helene's without them or their *culos* there every day. I would say, almost another year went by and then my grandfather finally pulled the plug. He only lived for about ten months after he retired but that was still a month longer than my grandmother.

He just couldn't make it without her and as he always did, he kept his promise to be with her forever. I could go on and on about their passing and how God knows how much that cut me and my family but this story is mostly about a book, and Mamma Grace, so I'll heartbreakingly leave that part there for now.

I heard the stories and even saw a few pictures of Mamma Grace when she was young, but I never met her until several months after my grandfather's funeral. She didn't attend either of my grandparent's funerals so how close she actually was to our family didn't come into full focus until I got to know her myself. Then it didn't take too long to understand.

I'll never forget the day I truly realized who she was. In very much the same spirit of my grandmother, this little older Italian woman busted through the restaurant doors and walked over directly to a pile of dishes.

Without a word to anyone she just started washing them. We were so busy at the time I didn't have time to address something that was more of a gift than a problem. Once things calmed down, I went over to basically thank her for the free help and also to find out who she was. Mamma Grace even looked like my grandmother in stature but definitely in attitude as well. She said, "Presley, I'm Grazia Isabella Russo, but you can call me Mamma Grace". I didn't know how she knew my name but after all the formalities, I finally realized who she was. I still didn't know why she was there at that time, or for that matter why she didn't come to either of my grandparents' funerals. I couldn't ask much though because she was doing most of the talking.

One thing that was obvious from the start was she was a hard worker just like both of my grandparents were. As the restaurant started getting a little busier again I felt I had to get my *culo* moving and do my part as well. She came in like she'd been there forever and somehow knew where to put up everything once it was cleaned. As closing time neared on her first day, she let me know that some time ago after my grandfather realized he wouldn't be able to, he asked her to come look out for me for a while. He somehow knew I wouldn't follow his wishes to sell the place, but Lord knows, how that lady achieved one of his other final requests by helping me as much as she did. If my grandmother was a fireball, Mamma Grace was a fireball times two or more, but she also had a lot of my grandfather's qualities about her. Being around Mamma Grace was a lot like having both of my grandparents back but this time it was with some pretty unique and sometimes quirky little twists.

OLD FRIENDS

I didn't necessarily think I needed help at the time but there was no way I could ever refuse the wishes of another very sassy and demanding little Italian woman nor from my grandfather. The thing about a restaurant that has been around as long as Heline's has been, is there are definitely regulars. Those are the people who are going to come in regardless of what's going on in the world. The apocalypse could hit and there would still be someone in there asking for a cup of coffee or a slice of pecan pie. The odd thing was Mamma Grace already knew quite a few of the older regulars and God knows they were excited to see her once again. Come to find out she and eight or nine of them grew up together after she came to the States with my grandparents. Every one of those sometimes rude and obnoxious men treated Mamma Grace like she was absolute royalty from the moment they reunited.

By name, there was Paul, Erick, Wyatt, Greg, Luke, Scott, and George. Before Mamma Grace arrived, even though I am a little ashamed to say it, I would cringe a little when I noticed a few of those men coming in. But after Mamma Grace's arrival, I don't know what magical spell she had over them, but they weren't the same. They were better people when she was around, or either they were some of the best actors I've ever seen.

I know I shouldn't judge but in fairness to describe each, Greg was a very distinguished-looking older gentleman, and I say that term loosely, but it was obvious that he wanted everyone to know just how wealthy he was. He always had this freshly cut wavy silver hair and wore the finest suits. His crowning adornment, however, was one of the most expensive Rolex's ever made. He'd sit on one of the spinning bar stools and spin his watch around as much as the kids spun those sparkly red stools.

Everybody knew he owned one of the largest construction companies in the city and believe me he wanted everyone to know it too. Most of the time he kept his bill under five or six dollars but when he went to pay, he'd rifle through stacks of $10's and $20's just to make sure he always paid with a $100 bill. When I saw him come in, I'd always have to send someone to the bank as fast as I could to make sure we had enough change for him when he was ready to leave. The other thing I could guarantee from his visits was even though he had a $10,000 or more watch on, he'd always complain about the prices. On rare occasions, he'd bring his wife, or his team of crooked lawyers in with him. I guess those were times he needed to feel more justified in his complaints and desired a crowd to support his displeasure.

You could tell he was the boss of his world but more so he wanted everyone to feel he was the king of theirs. As many do in small places, people talk and Greg had his fair share of hardships, especially concerning his family, but it was always so difficult for me to feel bad for him based on the way he acted and how he presented himself to others. I think everyone just presumed he was more concerned with making his money than he was about taking care of others, so to me, I thought, that's what he got. I almost thought he'd never return this one time, and probably secretly wished he wouldn't. But I raised the prices across the board by twenty-five cents and even though that little price increase was well past due you would have thought I called his mother a bad name or smacked him right across the face because my tiny adjustment just didn't settle well with him. He stayed away for about a solid month, but he did go around to all the other neighborhood establishments telling them how appalled he was.

Even before I committed that terrible atrocity, his wife would come with him more often. She'd usually only get a bowl of soup and as many crackers as she could eat. I'm sure that was because the crackers were free but after a while, we rarely ever saw her. I'm thinking the combined expense was just too much in his eyes. In fairness, I did see him slip people a few dollars every now and then, but with that man, you truly never knew if you were going to get the prince or the pauper, and the latter was by far the most prevalent.

The next regular, who was one of Mamma Grace's old friends, was Scott. Scott was Greg's polar opposite in many ways, and that doesn't necessarily mean in a good way. Scott never really wanted to do anything but sit around the restaurant all day. He'd listen to the music, work on a crossword puzzle, or read a book for hours on end. Scott evidentially didn't work and I'm not sure he ever did. He had some of the most peculiar eating habits because regardless of how good our variety of Italian food or barbecue was the only thing he ever ordered was liver. Out of everything to eat, especially at our little place, he always ate liver. I never understood his daily selection. Along with that peculiar desire, Scott always looked like he and his clothes were about a month past due for a good old-fashioned bath too. Most of his pants had duct tape stuck across a hole or a rip and many of his shirts had tears in them.

I probably should have taken that one particular delicacy off the menu and possibly could have fixed that problem, but regardless of how uncouth he could be at times, he really wasn't a bad guy. I knew Scott still lived with his mother even at his age and never married or had children. Part of me felt sorry for the guy but another part made me feel like that could be me if I wasn't careful. Of course, without the liver. He'd often talk about the military and his love for planes even though everyone knew he never served. I have to say though, he was extremely knowledgeable about his selected topics. He also loved watches and would sometimes go over to Greg to admire his. Greg never gave him the time of day, but I'd still bet that Scott knew more about Greg's watch than Greg did.

Back then I always wore my grandfather's watch. Now, my grandfather would never spend too much money on anything so frivolous, so it was just an old Timex that he had for years. To Scott for some reason, he felt my watch was as nice as Greg's and always commented on how much he'd like to buy it from me. I don't know if he was just talking or if he really meant it but it sure did seem like he was serious. With almost every visit Scott tried to get me to sell him my grandfather's watch but of course, I'd always somewhat politely decline. Again, for me, it was another tangible item to remember my grandfather by. I couldn't see myself ever getting rid of it. My grandfather gave me that watch right after our last conversation so regardless of its true monetary value, it was priceless to me.

To this day, if I close my eyes and think back just a little, I can still feel his hands when he put that watch on me. I feel that rough skin on those massive paws that provided so much for me and my family. But most of all I feel the love and compassion those hands helped deliver. At that point, I honestly felt that I'd never let that watch go but somehow in some way, my grandfather himself was the one who changed my mind. Again, people talk and one day we found out that Scott's mother died. I just knew, or at least assumed that she was probably the only person he ever really had in life. I knew he had to be feeling pretty lost at that time, and besides again, he really wasn't a bad guy. I don't know why, or how, and I can't give myself any credit for what happened next but it was almost as if I heard my grandfather's gentle yet bold voice telling me it was time to let it go. At first, I thought it was a heavenly message about the restaurant again, but it wasn't, it was about the watch.

I didn't actually hear any words, and if I did, it couldn't have been much more than a faint whisper. I think it was of a knowing that such a simple gesture might just help someone who had to be hurting pretty badly at that point. The next time Scott came in I had the watch ready for him with a sympathy card signed by everyone in the restaurant. His loss was something that I could definitely relate to and regardless of any of what many see as flaws, including that ridiculous liver fetish, I guess we at Helene's were the only family he had left. My grandparents in their many speeches of guidance, always reminded me that "stuff was just stuff." I laugh thinking back to some of those lessons because they always had a simple yet profound way of getting me to understand what they were trying to teach me.

They never wanted me to get too attached to material things because such things have a way of easily disappearing, especially the ones you hold on to the tightest. Scott was truly grateful for his gift. You would have thought I gave him a million dollars. I knew it was just a watch, but to him, it was so much more. That was the first time in a long time that I felt I did something right. I knew where to give the credit, but it still felt good. After his mother's passing, we discovered that he actually did eat other types of food. It wasn't too often but it did happen. He still had the duct tape and the ripped clothes but to me at least it just wasn't as noticeable as before.

Getting back to the men, and reverting back to my negativity, Paul was another one of Mamma Grace's old friends who unfortunately was also a regular. Again, he was the opposite of the others, but he wasn't any better. He was so loud and obnoxious, and he always told these off-color jokes, mostly about women, that no one wanted to hear. I could tell it made everyone around him feel uncomfortable by the looks on their faces. From a physical perspective, Paul was hard not to notice as well. He played college football back in his heyday and for an older man, he was still quite stout. To me, he still looked like he could tackle a few people now if he wanted to. Paul was good for business in the financial sense because he'd always eat a hearty meal and usually have at least one and sometimes two desserts after.

Paul was retired from some big insurance company, and I think he had plenty of money himself. Nowhere near as much as Greg but you could tell he wasn't hurting any. I heard Paul had been married more than a few times and definitely considered himself as the local Romeo. He brought many different women into the restaurant and no matter whether skinny, fat, short, or tall, Paul claimed to love them all. Those were his words, not mine. The worst thing about Paul was how opinionated he was, and he always made sure anyone who was around could hear his thoughts. Just like Greg with the Rolex, for attention, Paul barked out so many loud and absurd statements that sometimes those around him would leave in frustration. He always seemed to feel he was right about everything way before anyone ever asked his opinion on anything. He'd even frustrate George at times and George hardly ever got frustrated about anything.

George wasn't like the others. He was another one of Mamma Grace's old friends who came in every day. Like Scott, he stayed there most of each day too. As good as Paul was for business George was even better because he'd eat three or four times a day, and they were always big meals. George had to be well over three hundred pounds himself, but that was a different kind of weight than my grandfather carried. He almost took up one whole side of a booth all by himself. Much different from several of the others, George was at least humble. I think he was more worried about his next meal than getting any attention from those around him. I still have no idea how any human could eat that much food in a day. To make matters worse he hardly ever got up from his seat. He'd just sit in this one particular booth all day and order two pounds of barbecue here, three hamburgers there, and then later repeat with something similar. It was crazy to see how much that man could consume.

George didn't only like food though he liked to drink too. With some of my past in mind, it was a little hard for me to judge him about that, but I still did. After we'd close, he'd head down to the local bar. I guess since he ate all day, he felt that he needed to drink all night to wash it down. Again, people talk, and we knew he was medically retired from somewhere but I didn't know where or why. Like with many of the regulars, you get to know them a little. They often tell you about their lives, well at least the parts they wanted you to know. With George, he often told the same story repeatedly. Once again, whether I wanted to accept it or not, his life reminded me a little of mine. He told us about how he married his high school sweetheart. I didn't get that far with Isa but like me, he lost her somewhere along the way. I even knew her name from his stories, Becky. George would reminisce to whoever was around as if he and Becky were still together. It was kind of sad but I knew in some ways I was doing the exact same thing.

I don't know what he meant by it but he said she left him because he just wouldn't do what he was supposed to do. I might not have known but it was obvious that George knew exactly what she meant and from the sounds of it, never had any interest in moving on either. Once again, I realized that those at Helene's were probably his only family. George by no means was ever rude or pushy. He was somewhat somber, and he did have a sense of humor. He'd joke and play with every kid that came into the restaurant. He often spoke about how he wished he and Becky had children. Anyone could tell how lonely George was and how he was trying to fill all that emptiness with so many things.

I always felt that I had to include him in any of the special dinners or holiday functions, not only because again quite frankly in many ways I could relate but also because I just plain felt bad for the guy. One of these inclusions was our annual Thanksgiving dinner. Years ago, my grandparents started the tradition of giving away free Thanksgiving meals. They served any and everyone who wanted to join. Many people showed up with a dish of their own, but it was another wonderful thing passed along from my grandparents that I wanted to continue. On that day each year, George would throw on one of those puffy white chef's hats, one that I'd never wear, but he'd help us serve all day long. On those days he never worried about eating or drinking himself he was truly there to help others, and it was obvious and appreciated.

Thanksgiving wasn't the only day that George would become that inspired though. Every Christmas Eve he'd dress up like Santa Claus and believe me he fit the part too. He looked exactly like what I'd think old St. Nick would. It was almost as if George was a different person on those special days. He was gentle and kind to all of us and especially to the children who were so excited to see him. I will say we all truly enjoyed and appreciated those heart-warming kinds of days at the restaurant. George would almost immediately revert back to his old ways when those times were over, but we all knew how special at least those two days of the year were for him.

HELP

The next man to describe, who was the most different from the others was Wyatt. He was about six foot two inches and he also had long white hair and an even longer white beard, but he didn't look anything like Santa Claus. He was a fairly stocky man with tattoos from head to toe. He usually came into the restaurant only about once or twice a week, more after Mamma Grace got there but he always looked like he was mad at the world and would dare anyone to say anything to him about it. He never did anything wrong, but he sure did look like he could. For the most part, except for Mamma Grace, everyone would leave him alone and let him eat in peace. Some of those etched images on that man were on the verge of being horrifying. I had a tattoo myself, I got mine for what I thought was a tribute to some of my military friends who didn't make it home from the war.

I understood that tattoos, as well-meaning as they may be, can also be a self-inflicted punishment for living while others didn't. If that's the case Wyatt's tattoos must have some very serious stories to tell themselves. Especially the ones across the fingers on his right hand. They spelled out H-E-L-P. I felt pretty positive Wyatt's tattoos were from a prison somewhere. I could just picture a sharpened toothbrush etching those images directly into his soul. I wasn't sure what he needed help from, or who he was trying to send that message to, but that particular tattoo across his fingers was sincere enough to give me the chills.

They were rarely in the restaurant at the same time but if they were I could see Paul and Greg both side-eye Wyatt. They never spoke as far as I saw. It was weird that Mamma Grace was so much of a common denominator between all of those men because each couldn't be any more different than the other. I will say, even Wyatt and all of his tattoos would perk up and smile when Mamma Grace was around. Sometimes they'd even go over to a booth and sit and talk amongst themselves for quite a while. Wyatt seemed as happy as anyone during those times. Mamma Grace always treated everyone the same anyway. Everyone would become so relaxed around her and her magic. That woman wasn't as direct as my grandfather, nor quite as sassy as my grandmother. She was more like the perfect blend of each, and it looked like she didn't have to try very hard to be that way.

Again, I know I am not supposed to judge but some of Mamma Grace's old friends didn't get the subliminal message about how they were supposed to act in that little restaurant. But out of all of the guys who obviously had a shared past and acted so differently around Mamma Grace was Erick. To me, he was the most confusing. Erick and his wife Mary were also regulars. He usually came in several times a day and at least one of those times Mary would accompany him. I think he mostly came in to see what other people were doing. Mary wasn't quite as bad as Erick on the nuisance scale but she wasn't far off either. He was one of those know-it-alls but do a little kind of people. I'm not sure whether he ever had a regular job either. From what I heard if he needed money, he'd just get into his next car accident or fall in the supermarket. Again, I have to laugh because I can just picture an announcement saying pick up on aisle three.

I was always a little nervous when Erick and Mary came in because my insurance premiums were already high enough. I'd give him free tea or something similar just to keep his legal thoughts on my side. Erick and Mary didn't have any children, but twice a year on our special days, Thanksgiving and Christmas Eve, they would bring in their great nephew with them. His name was Mark, and he was somewhere around my age, but obviously much more successful. I was told he was a professional golfer, or at least trying to become one. He was able to travel around the world playing a sport that he was pretty darn good at. When Mark joined the pair Erick would always pay for the meals of everyone in the restaurant at the time. I don't know if that was because he was so happy to see his nephew, or if he was showing off his pretend riches but either way both Erick and Mary seemed to be a lot more reserved and happier when their nephew was around.

The final man from Mamma Grace's past to talk about was Luke. He also came in from time to time, but I really didn't know him that well, not that I knew any of the others but so well, but I knew Luke even less. Luke still had a high and tight from an obvious military past. His clothes, although not overly fancy, were always crisp and pressed with that perfect crease. That's kind of how I knew he was ex-military. Later my thoughts were verified through some of our brief conversations. He was a tall man with thick leathery skin but what was most memorable was his piercing blue eyes. That man had that numbness in his gaze.

I found out later that he was in both the Korean War and Vietnam. Although I went through hell, I knew his military experience was so much worse. Regardless of his appearance, he was surprisingly soft-spoken. When he did speak, he didn't seem to waste any words but some of our brief conversations got a little deep. I guess because he knew I was in a war there was a certain amount of trust given to me based on our commonality. I still wish he didn't tell me but one of the things he said was when he came back from Vietnam, he didn't feel fit enough to be around his two daughters or his wife, so he never was again. I've seen suicides, killings, and what I'd call murder all in the name of what some call war, but I couldn't imagine what Luke saw. I was so sorry about the price he had to pay. Anyway, he was another one who came in quite a bit more often after Mamma Grace arrived. I could tell he needed her too, maybe even more than the rest of us.

Again, like I've always said there are some days in the restaurant life you love and some you simply hate, but either way as hard as I tried and regardless of what the days brought, I still couldn't understand how Mamma Grace had so much control over these guys. I didn't find out until a little later that the reason she couldn't make it to either of my grandparent's funerals was because her husband was also sick at the time. He passed away not long after my grandfather so I guess her coming to Richmond was a way to help herself too. One of the good things about restaurant life is that even though we were mostly busy, there were definite downtimes each day. Those were the times when we were basically all caught up and pretty much had nothing else to do but talk and wait for someone else to come in. Those daily talks made it easy for me to feel like I knew Mamma Grace forever as well. She just had that special something about her. I knew and could tell that a lot of what I believed was so special was the obvious influence my grandparents had on her life, just like they did mine.

She may have been older, but she was still a beautiful woman both inside and out. I could picture Isa looking similar in her later years. I just knew Mamma Grace's family back in Italy considered her as their guiding light too. She often spoke about them. She talked about her children and grandchildren. She even told stories about her extended family, nieces, and nephews, some of whom were close to my age. God knows they had to be missing that woman, but I was so happy she was there with me, and I know all of her friends were too. We made a pretty good duo running that little place together, especially when I listened to her about how to run it.

M. A. COLE

GASTON

There would never be a day that restaurant didn't remind me of my grandparents but with Mamma Grace there at least it seemed manageable and sometimes even a little fun again. Before my grandfather died, he called me next to him and told me he was leaving the restaurant to me, but he wanted me to sell it and go find my own life. I never intended to take it over but at that time I just couldn't think about selling it either. He knew full well what that place provided for our family, but he also knew what it took away. In his words, the restaurant stripped him of time to do other things.

He said he regretted not taking time to travel or revisiting my grandmother's homeland. He wished he lived more of his life outside of that restaurant but he never did. Again, he was just always too busy building their humble little dynasty. After hearing such words, I pretty much defended him against himself. I never wanted to hear him have regrets about anything, especially after giving his family such a beautiful life. It didn't matter what I said though, he wanted more for my life, and he made that point as clear as he could before he had to go and be with my grandmother once again.

This was one order from my grandfather I just didn't have the heart to follow. To me, that place was an actual part of both of my grandparents and after their passing, I would have done anything to feel their presence again. I decided to pick them up at the restaurant where they left off. I often spoke to Mamma Grace about that last conversation I had with my grandfather and his actual wishes for me. This was one of the few topics she never really had much to say about, at least not at first. She'd always end those talks reminding me that sometimes we don't make our own plans. Sometimes somebody has a higher calling for our lives. I didn't know whether she was supporting my decision or politely telling me I was an idiot, but as my grandmother did, she'd also give out a cute little giggle and start working on something else as to say enough talking now get your *culo* moving.

With her there, as far as the restaurant itself went things were starting to normalize anyway. The place was finally once again running like a well-oiled machine. I thought since I was more or less the new engine in that machine, I better keep my mind clear of such thoughts anyway. I knew my grandfather just wanted me to have more freedom than he did, I fully understood that and probably wanted the same for myself, but I also felt that place was all I had left of those wonderful people, and I couldn't see any better way of honoring them.

After Mamma Grace had been at the restaurant for about four months or so, I guess just like when we had downtime in the desert, my mind started wandering again. Life didn't sting as bad as it once did, but I still thought about my grandparents every day. I thought about my military friends, and I still thought about Isa. I'd often wonder where she was and what she was doing. I figured by then, as wonderful as she was, she was probably out there living my dream with someone else but mostly I prayed that she was happy and safe. I tried so many ways to find that girl but nothing ever worked. It was like "Where's Waldo" before they even inserted the image on the page. She was absolutely nowhere to be found.

The same men from Mamma Grace's past started coming in even more than ever. She'd always talk to them individually, and they'd always behave while she was around. I'm not sure all her wishes for them to change in certain ways were taking hold though. I knew she was doing it out of love but many times towards the end of her conversations with those men they would leave with their heads down. She'd nonchalantly tell Paul or Greg or any of us for that matter to quiet down or humble up then a little discussion about her request would follow. She didn't spare anyone to include me. Most of what she guided me about was my judgment toward her older friends and others. Each time it was almost as if Mamma Grace was the parent that no one wanted to disappoint, but for some reason, all of us still did. She didn't say that in so many words, but we knew. We all knew including Paul, who got a little more of the other side of Mamma Grace than the rest of us at times.

For me, like I said my mind was wandering a bit, but I still wanted to make my new so-called business partner happy. One of the things other than Mamma Grace being there that I truly must be given credit for was my writing. Somewhere along the line, I started writing down these stories about my imaginary life with Isa among other things. We'd go on these adventures to exotic islands, or climb some of the highest mountains. That particular story still makes me laugh because I don't even like heights. But I would get so lost in my own words that I physically felt like I was wherever I wrote about. I can't explain the feelings that writing created without including the word free. Some stories were about doing things with my military buddies or surprising my grandparents with that trip back to Italy. Eventually I found myself writing every chance I got because I felt so unbound and again believe me running a restaurant can bind you up. I'd even get up in the middle of the night at times to write something that I suddenly and inconveniently thought of. I guess I was too scared I'd forget it by morning.

I'm not sure how healthy it was living in this fictional world but even with still having the restaurant this may have been at least part of that freedom my grandfather always wanted for me. I rarely ever went back and read what I wrote. I think that was because I already knew the stories so well. Hell, I was the one making them all up. Hours and hours were spent writing all of the dreams I had for my life. It really was as if they were already happening. Line by line my pain had reduced to only remembering mostly the good times. It was an unexpected escape, one that I would never have known how to plan for myself. Of course, I still worked a lot and had to have my daily conversations with Mamma Grace, but I would also become lost in that world that I created in my mind and then on paper.

Funny enough I even made those men I still sometimes cringed at the main characters of some of my stories.

The stories kept coming and I'd get more consumed by what they were becoming. My favorite story though as you would guess was about my Isa. Yes, before I wrote about where we'd go and what we'd do, almost like a somewhat creative pity party but this one story was different. It was as if God himself whispered the words for me to write down. I was careful not to feel too blessed though, because I thought I'd been down that road before but I was still very grateful that this particular story was dictated from above. I had to do little more than put my pen to the paper while following the directions of those gentle whispers. I couldn't stop writing if I wanted to, but either way, I didn't want to. I will say, that is one story that I still read over and over again. I let Mamma Grace read it too.

Laughingly, I think she was as shocked as I was that I could write something like that but again in truth, it wasn't me. I named, or should I say the true author titled that precious story with just a few delicately whispered Italian words, *"Sempre E Per Sempre."* I'm not exaggerating when I say I had to look up what those words meant in an English dictionary. I almost cried when I discovered it meant "Forever and Always" in English. The title alone was one of the greatest gifts I'd ever received.

Since I felt so strongly that what had been written was otherworldly or even divine, I knew it was also a gift for others.

I was so happy and content with what I was given that I paid a young college student fifty dollars to type it up. I then had 100 copies made and bound as a real book would be. I left the copies near the restaurant's register so anyone who wanted could take one. I got a few sarcastic comments, especially from some of Mamma Grace's older friends calling me the old man in the sea, after Hemmingway. But once I reminded them that I was more than half their age they cut it out. They would have stopped making fun of me sooner if Mamma Grace had gotten to them first. I will say George out of everyone was the most appreciative. Again, he was always there and had nothing else to do other than eat so he had plenty of time to read a book. He read "Forever and Always" from cover to cover in one setting. I think the way the other men acted toward me after the original ribbing showed they all read it too.

I definitely didn't quite have the same power to humble those men as Mamma Grace did but I think they could see their own lives in that book. The good, the bad, the happy and the sad. The heartbreak of missed opportunities and also the great blessings in life were all included. It was all there and just so relatable to everyone. I still would never take credit though. I didn't even use my name when I signed the bottom as Mamma Grace said I should. Instead, where the author's name usually went, I simply wrote the words "Thank you." I finally knew that regardless of how my life goes it doesn't mean there isn't something to be learned, and there's always something to be thankful for. That little self-printed book got quite a bit of notoriety at the restaurant. I gave away all 100 copies and I think it served its purpose for me and for whomever it may have reached.

I still wrote quite a bit after that. I even still hear the whispers from time to time but as of yet, it's never been as pronounced as that one time. Mamma Grace tried to talk me into sending that makeshift book to a publisher, but I honestly felt that I did what I was supposed to do with it, kind of like I was doing at the restaurant, and both decisions served their purpose. Restaurants as they do, come and go. That particular restaurant, Helene's, had been around for a long time, and it was more like another cranky old man more so than an aged fine wine. Things would break and we'd fix them but nothing and I mean nothing ever stopped those doors from opening. Well, that is until this one freakishly ridiculous storm that someone named Gaston came through. I got pretty good at looking things up due to all of that writing so I wanted to know what the word Gaston meant. Storms are usually named after people but Gaston from what I found, meant foreign warrior.

That storm may not have been foreign because it hit our neighborhood, but it was definitely a warrior against Mother Nature. It began about daybreak, right after Mamma Grace and I arrived at the restaurant. Within no time there was so much flooding around all four sides of that little building it seemed Helene's had turned into its own island. The wind blew and the rain poured throughout the day and well into the night. It flooded everything around but thankfully not very much water made its way inside. Since she had been in Richmond, Mamma Grace had been staying with another one of her old friends who I'd seen in the restaurant a few times but not many. We called her Diamond Lil.

Again, with the nicknames and I guess judgment. This woman dressed on the same level as Greg but with that female flair. The few times she'd been in the restaurant she looked like she was going to a grand ball more so than a very modest little eating establishment. Diamond Lil even let Mamma Grace borrow one of her cars to come to work every day. It was kind of funny seeing this little bitty Italian woman getting out of that great big shiny silver Cadillac. I don't think Diamond Lil, whose real name, by the way, is Elizabeth ever wanted Mamma Grace to work, she would have paid for everything, but Mamma Grace knew she was on a mission, and it wasn't just for me. It was a mission to help all of her older friends and herself along the way. If Diamond Lil wasn't careful, she'd get her too.

Either way, I tried to get Mamma Grace home before the storm got too bad, to Diamond Lil's house anyway. I knew we could get that Cadillac home another time, but it was no use. First, we went north but quickly ran into what looked like a river of water. Then we went east, west, and south but it was no use. We were lucky enough to get back to the restaurant even though the power was already out. I quickly found a few flashlights and a battery-powered radio. It didn't take long for us to realize that we might as well settle in because we weren't going anywhere anytime soon. To confirm our thoughts, the emergency broadcasts ordered everyone to stay off the roads.

As bad as it was, I knew there were many worse places to be trapped in other than a dry restaurant full of food. At first, Mamma Grace and I played cards to pass the time but after she beat me four or five times in a row it was obvious that she wanted to talk instead of play games. If I didn't know better, I would almost think that little woman set that storm up for her own purposes. She knew I still judged many of her friends and she wanted to set the records straight. As she said, she wanted to give me the rest of the story as Paul Harvey would say. I didn't know who Paul Harvey was but if Mamma Grace wanted me to do something I'm sure that's what I had to do. I listened to every word throughout the rest of the day and most of the night. We'd take a break every now and then to fix a sandwich or get a drink, but she knew she had a captive audience because we couldn't do anything else.

M. A. COLE

TOUGH TIMES

She started with Greg. She knew I thought he was one of the most greedy and arrogant men I'd ever met but she'd immediately stop me if I uttered such things. She let me know that Greg grew up in utter poverty himself. Like my grandfather, the only clothes they ever had were made out of feed sacks until much later in life. Greg's parents told their children that they had to go out of town for a funeral and never came back, well not for a long time anyway. He was no more than thirteen years old when he inherited the responsibility of taking care of his two younger sisters. Greg raised his sisters as a child himself. People in the area who knew about their situation helped when they could but taking care of two younger siblings as a child himself was a lot. Not finishing school wasn't rare back then but even at that time Greg had to quit school earlier than most. He had to make sure he could work enough to take care of his sisters as well as give them what he thought they deserved. With him being so young it was hard to find a decent job.

Mamma Grace was obviously a very special young lady back then too. When she came across an old tractor that someone had discarded, all she could think about was telling Greg where it was and how it could possibly help his particular situation. Mamma Grace said neither she nor Greg had any clue how to get that thing running, but Greg loved the idea so much that Mamma Grace got my grandfather to help. I felt like tearing up listening to her story. Maybe it was because it reminded me of how wonderful my grandfather was, or perhaps it made me consider how hard Greg had it. Either way, I discreetly wiped my eyes and gave Mamma Grace my full attention. All of this new information was coming full circle, and I began to understand why Greg admired Mamma Grace so much.

My grandfather not only got that old tractor running, but he also taught Greg about all of its parts and pieces. Coming from such an impoverished background himself, my grandfather couldn't afford to get help many times, so he had to learn a little bit about everything. Greg never looked back. He secured grading jobs and came up with numerous other ways to make money with that tractor. Often, he was chosen over much older men who had better equipment but lacked his determination and sometimes literal hunger. Greg accomplished every job to perfection, and it wasn't long before his reputation spread, regardless of his age. One old tractor led to two new ones, followed by a bulldozer and a dump truck. Before long, he had established an impressive construction company. Not only did he provide a better life than most for his sisters, but he also sent both of them to college. Such an accomplishment was a true rarity for those times, even among the richest families.

As I listened to Mamma Grace explain Greg's early years, I understood that those were tough times. What I didn't get was why he remained so sour despite his success. My curiosity led me to ask. Mamma Grace revealed that once his parents heard of his success, they decided to return home to claim a share of his newfound prosperity. Prior to their return, Greg didn't even know if his parents were alive. He had been handling his adult responsibilities for years. However, when they returned home, they expected, and even demanded repayment for rent on the shack they left him and his sisters in. That, along with more money for the debt they accumulated while they were gone. It was a definite reminder that not everyone is born into a loving family. Thinking about my own upbringing, I never imagined anything like what Greg experienced was possible.

After listening to his parents' demands it made him bitter but it also made him work harder than ever before. He wanted to be able to afford to get himself and his sisters away from them forever. I instantly had a different opinion of Greg because I don't think I would have been as persistent or even tough enough to do what he did. I knew that was a different time but what his parents did wasn't right regardless of the era. Mamma Grace did say that his bitterness and even appearances of greed towards others had gone too far. She wanted to help him become free from those traits. As she did quite often, she giggled and told me it's okay though, she had a plan.

If that was Greg's story, I didn't know if I wanted to hear anyone else's. That one was rough, but her talks weren't gossip. They were Mamma Grace's attempt to correct me to know enough to stop judging her friends, because as she said, no one really knows anyone else's story unless they were there, and she was there with all those men throughout her childhood.

Paul was the next she spoke about. I think she started with my least favorites first, but Paul also went to school with Mamma Grace. He went the whole way through though. She said that boy asked her out every single month in high school but the only place she'd go with him was the library. I laughed and was thankful Mamma Grace wasn't getting ready tell me a story about some old romance with that guy.

She said Paul has always acted so overly confident mostly to cover up a true lack of confidence. For him, those feelings come and go. Back then no one ever tested for learning disabilities and although he was a remarkable football player he almost failed off the high school team several times. Paul's parents were stern people, especially his father. His father just thought Paul was lazy and would often scold him to the point of tears or worse, but that wasn't all. After I heard Mamma Grace's story about Paul, I realized she was the reason he eventually got a scholarship to play football in college. She never directly said it but I would have been an idiot not to understand how she was involved in each of these men's early lives.

Mamma Grace was walking to school one day, and even though Paul's father was much smaller than he was she saw him beating Paul with a belt. Again, that was a different time, but as nosey as little Mamma Grace had to have been then too, she felt she just had to know what was going on. She didn't find out when it was happening for fear of getting whipped herself but when she saw Paul at school she asked. He opened up to her about his issues with learning. Mamma Grace wasn't even a native American, but she took to the language and her studies so wonderfully that she was always at the top of her class, so she agreed to tutor him. Once a week they'd meet in the school's library and even though Mamma Grace said Paul wanted more, she said smarter is all he got. I was still sitting there picturing those romantic attempts from Paul towards Mamma Grace but for some reason, I was imagining them at their ages now. I laughed envisioning Paul trying all that player-player stuff on our Mamma Grace.

Mamma Grace went on to say he did eventually do well on his own, but he did have one backslide that almost cost him his college career and some more skin off of his backside. Paul was scheduled for the college entrance test on this one particular Thursday. If he didn't do at least fair on that test, no school in the country would have paid for his education no matter how good he was at football. He didn't do poorly on the test because he didn't even show up. When Mamma Grace said when she found out she was livid. She had worked so hard with him so he'd have opportunities that so few others had at the time, and he just threw it away. She was so pissed she went to the testing coordinator and made up some story about Paul being sick and got the test rescheduled for the next day. Not only did she get the test rescheduled, but she also headed to Paul's house to tell his father what he had done. She said at that time she could have almost beat him with a belt herself.

I even knew not to mess with an angry Italian lady no matter what age they were. While Mamma Grace was headed to talk to Paul's father, her realization was Paul had the knowledge to do well on the test because she helped him, but the actual problem was he was scared. In her thinking, he felt he couldn't fail if he didn't show up regardless of what it cost him. Again, very few people went to college back then, especially from where they lived. She thought he just didn't understand how good of an opportunity going to college was. By the time she got to Paul's house instead of telling his father that he'd already missed one testing opportunity she only told the part about the test being the next day.

Mamma Grace would bend the rules and maybe even the truth a little if she thought it would help someone. Anyway, while Mamma Grace was relaying the message to Paul's father Paul arrived home. She said his face turned as red as a radish after he saw her because he knew that she knew he had skipped the test. Paul assumed she was there to tell his father but again that's not exactly what happened. Paul's father nonchalantly told Paul about his test date, thanked Mamma Grace for the message, and went inside their house. Paul then knew she didn't tell on him but he also knew she would knock him out herself if he missed it again. Mamma Grace had already taken the test so she knew exactly what was on it and stayed an extra hour studying with him under an old oak tree. She knew he could pass and before she left, she had Paul believing it too. When the test scores came back, they were both right and he was offered a full ride to one of the best colleges in the state. He started on the Varsity team all four years and did very well on the field but also in the classroom.

Paul was never lazy, he just had bouts of not believing in himself, and that in her opinion is why he was so boisterous at times. He had so many people tell him how great he was when he was playing football but those kinds of things never last. In other words, he needed to take his eyes off himself and learn how to help others. Mamma Grace said that's where true happiness and satisfaction comes from anyway. Again, when she felt she had said all she needed to say about someone she'd somewhat deviously giggle and say it's okay though, I have a plan. Mamma Grace didn't seem like she was playing about those plans she kept mentioning. I could envision her standing over each one of those men rubbing her hands together getting ready to unleash some of that magical Mamma Grace juju over them.

The true source of her power was becoming a little clearer to me. It wasn't anything magical, it was just plain love. When she saw someone in need, she didn't hold back; she did something about it. A lot of times that something was pretty magical, but you still have to give love the credit. I told you that lady was fireball times two. If my eyes leaked a little thinking about Greg and his parents leaving him and his sisters, I was desperately trying to hang on to my self-perceived toughness when she started talking about Wyatt. As I expected Wyatt had been in prison. He was there for quite a while too. This story even had Mamma Grace in tears as she confirmed that Wyatt did kill a man.

So many people were so poor back then that some would do almost anything to get what they thought they needed. On this terrible day, a man came up to Wyatt and his new young wife and pulled a gun on them to rob them. They didn't have anything to take, and Wyatt complied with all of the man's requests but that wasn't good enough. That lost man shot Wyatt's wife and when he turned to shoot Wyatt rage set in. Wyatt killed that thief with his own bare hands. Mamma Grace never understood why that judge sent Wyatt to prison, but he did. My heart broke as Mamma Grace told Wyatt's story and on a much less serious note, I thought about what if my grandfather or myself had a judge like Wyatt had. How much different would our lives have been

Wyatt's wife's name was Sally. She also went to school with Mamma Grace, she was just eighteen years old. Mamma Grace knew Sally well and cried thinking about how Sally didn't deserve to have her life cut short by something so senseless, and about how Wyatt didn't deserve it either. You could visibly tell that story shook up Mamma Grace. I think again, people talk, and without knowing the circumstances Wyatt just became the local murderer to most in the town. Mamma Grace knew better and from the first week after Wyatt was sentenced, she wrote him. He didn't write back at first but as she does, Mamma Grace's got to him too. Even after she went back to Italy, she and Wyatt sent letters back and forth the whole time he was incarcerated and even up to the time she arrived at the restaurant. Wyatt went through something that the others didn't but either way, Mamma Grace once again said it's okay though I have a plan. That time she didn't giggle.

All this talk of death made me think of my grandparents, who were really her surrogate parents. I asked about how they were then. She smiled and told me that I already knew, but then let out that missing giggle. She told me how much fun she had growing up, and how cared for she felt. She said at first, she was a little scared of my giant grandfather but it didn't take long to realize how much of a teddy bear he was. She spoke about my grandmother like she was the most loving big sister. She said she never looked at my grandparents as her parents because she already had a mother and a father whether they were with her or not, but she did consider them as the most loving family a girl could have.

I was cracking up a little as she told me how at times, she and my grandmother would fuss a bit towards each other like most sisters do. I can only imagine how those feisty Italian spats went. She laughed when she said my grandmother always won. I could tell she loved my grandparents and that would always be enough for me. She then turned her thoughts to her own parents. I knew they were killed in the war but that's all I knew. Her father as she said was the apple of her eye. He was a smaller man and she remembered how he was always joking around playing his guitar and singing or doing almost anything else he could to amuse her. She was ten years old when they died, and she, as I can with my grandfather's hands, claimed to still be able to feel the stubble on his face from when he'd hug her.

Her mother as she described was a beautiful, elegant woman. They were poor too, but you'd never know it by the way her mother dressed or presented herself. She was often knitting or cooking, in many ways she was the boss of the family. Her mother was also the one who taught her to give back to others because often what she made whether it be food or crafts, she'd give away to the less fortunate. Both of her parents were kind and loving, they just showed it in different ways. Remember Italy and the United States were at war at the time however many Italians looked at the American soldiers as liberators and welcomed them. Both of her parents died in a bombing that tore up the town. Mamma Grace never knew which side it came from.

My grandmother's family lived on the outskirts of town, and they were already family friends so Mamma Grace ran to their house as fast as she could and never left until she came to the States. I realized just then that Mamma Grace understood war and its evils first hand too. Even though they died long before I was born Mamma Grace told me a little about my great grandparents too. My grandmother's mother and father. She said my great grandfather was one of the funniest men she had ever met. I guess because times were so hard Mamma Grace's father and my great grandfather did everything they could do to keep everyone's mind off of their surroundings and what was actually happening. She said my great-grandfather's name was Enzo and he'd have a bottle of wine in his right hand and the Bible in his left. Again, she laughed again as she said he used his right hand a lot more.

I'd seen old black and white pictures of my great-grandfather and I know I'm judging again but he looked the part. She remembered him as a worker. He'd basically work all day on their little farm and two fist in the afternoon, again using his right hand more. He was another storyteller and with so much going on around them he got everyone's mind off of their reality. Her father was my great-grandfather's best friend and when she first arrived, he was hurting almost as much as she was but he pulled himself together to ease her pain. My great-grandmother, similar to my grandparents, was described as another one who was very different from her spouse. Mamma Grace said at first, she thought my great-grandmother was strict but then she noticed most of her orders came with a wink.

They had a lot of people living in their small house, so Mamma Grace felt that my great-grandmother must have felt she needed to at least give the appearance of running a tight ship. My great-grandmother's name was Angelica. Mamma Grace confirmed that was the perfect name for her because she had the voice of an angel. She sang as much as my great-grandfather drank. Mamma Grace told me for the first few months after her arrival my great-grandmother would come to her room to sing to her so she could fall sleep. Of course, she'd wink before she started singing but the words to every song would soothe her soul and, at least for a while, take her mind off of her parents so her heart could rest.

I'd never heard any of these stories before and knowing the last few people she spoke about were related to me made me feel proud. I thought to myself, maybe I can blame my drinking years on my great-grandfather, but I didn't say it out loud. The storm outside still hadn't let up and Mamma Grace got up and *"Italianized"* a snack that I thought couldn't be any more Italian. We had both gelato and ice cream at the restaurant but I knew what she'd choose. She knew if we didn't eat it, most of it would probably melt, and we'd have to throw it away. Hey, I was mixed so I liked both but when she came out with two scoops of gelato for each of us, she also brought out the olive oil. I looked at that woman like she was off her rocker. I reminded her that we weren't eating salads or bread but she acted like she knew what she was doing and began to ruin our desserts.

She poured that olive oil all over her portion and then mine. I thought to myself, "What in the hell are you doing lady?" but dared not say it. I'll be honest, I thought that storm or us being trapped inside was starting to get to her medulla oblongata. She almost took offense for me not trusting her but once again what Mamma Grace wants Mamma Grace gets and I somewhat held my breath and took a bite. I don't know why it took Mamma Grace to show me what gelato should taste like, but she was right. I would have never guessed it in a thousand years but olive oil actually does make gelato taste even better. It was like my taste buds had their own fourth of July. I think that culinary experience was the comic relief that we both needed before she started speaking about her husband.

M. A. COLE

MUSTARD SEED

Mamma Grace was full of love, the same kind of love I've been so blessed to be around throughout my life, I've always felt that I hit the proverbial lottery when it came to my family and I knew she did too. Her husband's name was also Enzo, she assured me he wasn't a big drinker though. Enzo was just a common Italian name but he was the love of her life. She said he always made her feel like a princess even in his last days. He worked in the shipyard, and they moved back and forth between Palermo and Aviano. My ears perked up because I knew I told her I was based in Italy, but I don't think I ever told her that I was actually in Aviano myself. They have two daughters who are older than my parents and six grandchildren. She said her Enzo was a big man, almost as big as my grandfather and he had a heart much the same. She also said he could be a little snippy like my grandmother.

She spoke about his sense of humor as being very similar to her father and my great-grandfather, and that he had a voice not quite as good but close to my great-grandmothers. It sounded as if she picked someone with many of the best characteristics of those she loved the most. As she spoke about her family she smiled the whole time. I asked her if she missed them already knowing the answer, but she said she'd return to them when her plans were complete. Oh no, here we go with the plans again, I thought. As she told me about her husband's death, I don't think I've ever heard a description of someone's passing so eloquently relayed. She said it was his time to go to a much greater place and do much greater things. I'll be honest, how could anyone see death as a negative if we truly felt that way?

She confirmed that she talks to her daughters and grandchildren from Diamond Lil's house but of course, she called her Elizabeth. She also said that she keeps up with her family and they keep up with her too. Mamma Grace's elegance was on display when she spoke about her family. She let me know she had many nieces and nephews that she was very close with and they'd also call from time to time. Before long I felt a little guilty that she was there with me instead of being back home with her family but it sounds like she had a handle on everything, not that I should have thought any differently.

She began asking me about Isa and my book next. She knew most of my story, how I left for a war on the day I was going to ask her to marry me, and the fact that I still had her grandmother's wedding ring. She even knew that I'd tried in every way that I could to find her. Mamma Grace knew I was telling the truth because not only had she heard these stories before, but she read the book. She still thought I should send it to a publisher, but she didn't push me on that, at least not then. Then she said verbatim something she told me in one of our first conversations; sometimes we don't make our own plans. Sometimes somebody has a higher calling for our lives.

I told her I just wished my calling included Isa but I guess that somebody she spoke of had other plans. We both got up from the booth where we were sitting to stretch out and I washed the bowls we used for the olive oil gelato. I still can't believe that stuff was as good as it was, or that I'd never thought of doing that before. Once sitting back down she told me she wanted to talk to me about the restaurant and my grandfather's true wishes for me. This was a topic that I knew he spoke to her about but another she never pushed on until then. I told her things she already knew. I told her how I felt that restaurant was a literal part of my grandparents, and how I never could see myself selling it, of course unless I won the lottery.

She understood but then that doggone woman tried to trick me by telling a story about a man who gave a watch away that once belonged to his grandfather. I knew Scott and her, the recipient of my grandfather's watch, talked all the time. I didn't know where she was going with that story at first, but of course, a giggle came soon after. That was the first time she ever gave her opinions on what she felt I should do. She also felt I had too much living to get on with to be at the restaurant all the time. In her view selling that place would not only give me the money to do what she felt I needed to do but also the time. In her version of my life, I'd go to wonderful places like Italy again and just travel and write.

I thought for a minute she was going to throw in an Old Man in the Sea Hemmingway joke, as some of her friends did but she was serious. I had to somewhat tune her out at that point because her version of my life seemed much better than the one I was living but it just wasn't an option for me. Besides I haven't made any money writing, and I can't live off of sold restaurant money forever. I'd have to work somewhere and it would probably be worse than where I was. I wouldn't know how to act working a nine to five Monday through Friday instead of our wonderful shifts of 6 a.m. or earlier until after 9 p.m. almost seven days a week. When I said that out loud, I think I was proving Mamma Grace's point better than my own but she had to get the picture.

She could tell that I was a little bit touchy on that subject, so she finally got back to her friends. One story after the other kept clearing up why these men were the way they were and why Mamma Grace was so special to them. Make no mistake about it, even Mamma Grace realized they were all in need of a plan, but I definitely was starting to feel more compassion for all the men and later even for a few women. As Mamma Grace started talking about Erick, she also told me a little more about the times and how poor much of the country was. She reminded me that wealth and riches aren't the root of all evil but sometimes people's methods of obtaining it is. She said that she'd even seen kids for sale or abandoned like Greg and his sisters were. It was a different time and not necessarily better. In many ways it was more challenging and how those such as herself and me that hit that family lottery had to do all they could to pass it on.

I got a feeling that her analogies and history lessons were still being directed at me. Mamma Grace returned to Erick after and said that he grew up in an orphanage. Again, poverty was rampant but sometimes love wasn't. He didn't just grow up there, he spent most of his young life in that miserable place. Many times, the people there didn't treat him very kindly either. He was messed with in more ways than one. She didn't go into details, and I didn't ask but if there was the least little possibility of what I think she was talking about my heart goes out to him even more. It's crazy that people can have children and not care about them, I thought.

Erick always seemed to be looking to get something for free probably because he's never really had anything. Mamma Grace told me how Mary was in the same orphanage on the girl's side, and that's where they met. Unfortunately, they have more in common than meets the eye. Even though both kids lived in the home they still had to go to school and there was only one school around. Mamma Grace spoke of how badly they were treated at the home but also at school. She said she always made it a point to sit with those two at lunch and be as silly as she could to try and get their minds off of their reality. Mamma Grace said she usually got a few smiles but mostly she was there to make sure they didn't get picked on at least during their time together each day. My heart was breaking again when I listened to Erick and Mary's story but once again, she said it's okay though, I have a plan. Again, this was a giggle-less ending.

I thought all of their stories were so sad I might have to have another bowl of that olive oil gelato just to get through the last few. It had been somewhat dark outside all day due to the storm but by this time it must have been around 9 or 10 p.m. and there was absolutely no light from the night sky. It was almost ominous how dark it was outside but inside we kept going by candlelight. I wondered if George knew about the olive oil thing once Mamma Grace started talking about him. George was the big man who was basically eating and drinking himself to death. Mamma Grace said he was only doing what he saw growing up. He grew up with alcoholic parents and although they never beat him or left him, they were never there for him either. He got married right out of school and was happy for a while but the more he drank the less happy his wife was.

She couldn't handle it and left him. She came back several times trying to help him but she seemed to think he loved the bottle and the fork more than he did her. George's family were my grandparents' neighbors so Mamma Grace and George would walk to school together every day. George didn't start drinking until after he got older but he was always somewhat of a big kid. That alone was probably why some of the same little jerks that picked on Erick and Mary picked on him. Sometimes it was relentless, but George did feel safe when the little and big version of Mamma Grace were around.

Mamma Grace talked about this one time during the first snow of the year how those little brats didn't see her hiding, so they started pelting snowballs at George. George tried to fight back but he was a little clumsy and outnumbered. Those bad kids didn't realize Mamma Grace had a plan then too. She expected something like that to happen with all of that new snow. So, she left the house about an hour early and prepared twenty of the most beautiful round snowballs you would ever see and left them behind a tree to freeze and harden even more. Once George started getting hit Mamma Grace came out from behind that tree and started throwing what was the equivalent to a pound of solid ice at each of those kids. She said it was a slaughterhouse that day and giggled even louder again. She said she drew blood from every one of those bullies and at least that crew never picked on George again, and yes, she had a new plan for him this time too.

We talked a little bit about how well George did on our two special days, Thanksgiving and Christmas Eve, and how good and funny he was around children. She knew he wanted to change, he just hadn't been able to as of yet on his own. Quite frankly, she felt they were all running out of time. After George, she talked a little bit about aging in general. This part I knew would somehow revert back to selling the restaurant because her theme was going on to that better place to do better things without any regrets. I was always hoping those were just meaningless words that came out of my grandfather's mouth but she truly felt those were some of his last wishes. Up to that point she hadn't been as vocal about that topic but for some reason that night she started to be.

By then it was well into the night and the rain had slowed to little more than drizzle. The flooding all around was still there and we still couldn't go anywhere so I guess she felt she had to finish what she started. She didn't bring up the restaurant anymore that night but I knew part of her thoughts on dying without regrets were also directed at me. She told me that before her Enzo died, she sat down at his bedside and asked him if he had any regrets. He wasn't as quick to offer any up as my grandfather was and assured her, he didn't. In response she tricked him and then asked if he had to tell your best friend what would be the top three regrets to avoid, what would they be? I don't know if Enzo knew what Mamma Grace was doing or not, but he did play along.

Enzo said to always be true to yourself and don't necessarily do what others expect you to do. I thought to myself, *"well there's strike one for me"*. Then he said don't work so much, play more and have a life full of fun, everyone should spend more time with their friends and family having fun. I thought again, *"Okay, now I know that's at least strike two and three for me."* Then I subconsciously asked myself, "how many strikes do you get in this damn game anyway". According to Mamma

Grace, Enzo said his next thought was to have the courage to go out in the world and be who you are meant to be. I thought again, *"damn, strike four or fumble or whatever I'm up to now"*. She told me how after he ran down his list, he then smiled at her and said, "But like I said I have no regrets, so I hope my friend gets the message." I'll be honest I pray it's a long time from now but I don't think Mamma Grace should ever have any regrets when she goes to that much greater place to do much greater things either.

I was starting to get a little tired but Mamma Grace wasn't having it. She hadn't finished yet and she said there was still the story of Scott, Luke, and Elizabeth. I almost said Diamond Lil again, but I held back. I then ask how Elizabeth fits into this mix. She laughed and said "I'm going to save her for last because her Cadillac is about half underwater outside and I don't want to think about that yet". That time I laughed but fully understood and became more grateful that I had a truck with somewhat larger tires and the water hadn't reached inside yet. When she spoke about Scott knowing that it hadn't been long since his mother died, I knew this was going to be another tough one although it didn't start out that way.

Mamma Grace said Scott had very nice and loving parents. Scott always did even better than she did in school. He used to win all the science fairs and turn in the best work on school projects. He never really got picked on either. She knew he'd never been in the military, but she also knew he worked for a defense company for a while. He even invented some part for a jet, but the company stole his idea and fired him. As far as his childhood went, it was as good as anyone's until it wasn't. Scott's father was also an aeronautic fanatic and they'd sit up for hours after he should have been in bed talking about their shared favorite topic. His father owned a butcher shop but just like Scott his dad knew every new jet or plane and how they functioned.

Scott's mother worked in the cafeteria of the high school back then. Neither made very much money but she was one of the sweetest women and she always gave Mamma Grace an extra milk or dessert for kind of looking out for Scott even though she never really had to. Scott's father's business started failing. Those were tough times for everyone back then. He'd work more to try to make more but then the tax people started coming around. Not only did he owe his suppliers an amount he couldn't pay, he also owed the government. They were relentless. They even went to his house to threaten him about not paying, and eventually took the little money he had in the bank. It was just too much for him and Scott's father took his own life in that same little shop he was trying to save his family with.

Scott and his father were so close, Scott never got over it. Mamma Grace knew that Scott's father was just so confused and couldn't see a way out. That's the only explanation she could think of. Scott's mother didn't take it well either and afterward quit her job and rarely ever left the house again. Mamma Grace wasn't sure but she said she'd bet both the liver and my grandfather's watch must in some way remind him of his father. I sank a little thinking about how many times I made fun of his preferred food selection in my head.

When Mamma Grace found out what happened she knew that was one problem that was too big for even her, but she also knew where to ask for help. Every Sunday until she went back to Italy she took Scott to church. He didn't keep going after she left but she did say at least it looked like he had a little relief on the days they went. Mamma Grace didn't say anything about having a plan for Scott but I knew she'd never leave him out. Mamma Grace was so special. Since she was about the same size as Mother Teresa, I wondered if they were related. But as she spoke you could see the hurt in her own eyes as if all of those terrible things that happened to everyone else also directly happened to her too. I have had some wonderful people in my life, but I'd never met anyone like her, I thought.

She did let me get up and use the bathroom before she started on what I thought was the last combined story. That is one that I didn't see coming, not that I saw any of them coming in the way they did. But that last story reminded me of a twisted soap opera or a sadistic tele novella. I already knew Luke was ex-military. I felt I could relate but when I found out he was a prisoner of war in Vietnam I didn't feel like I could relate anymore. It's not a competition but Vietnam was one of the most violent wars the U.S. has ever been a part of even though it was never labeled as such. He was obviously released or freed in some way but Mamma Grace said he's been going back and forth to the Veterans Hospital trying to get all of that terror out of him ever since.

On the outside, he looks somewhat normal even pretty good for his age but on the inside, he must have those jagged edges that so many have from war. I guess the difference with his is because of what he went through his edges must be razor-sharp. Okay, now the shocking part. Luke himself told me that he never went back to his kids, who are now older than me or his wife, but I would have never guessed that his wife was Diamond Lil, I mean Elizabeth. My jaw dropped when I heard that. Again, like I said, a twisted soap opera. Both have been in the restaurant so they're both still in the area, but I had no idea. I don't know what plan Mamma Grace thinks she has with that one, but she still claimed to have one. Both Mamma Grace and I had had enough by then and we stretched out the best we could to try and get at least a little sleep. We were both hoping to get off of Helene's island by morning.

Right before we fell asleep, Mamma Grace put the nightcap on the evening by reassuring me that regardless of how the situations may have seemed in all those stories, God was there. He was with those men and the two ladies, Elizabeth, and Mary, and He's there with us too. God is everywhere. He covers everyone no matter whether they accept His eternal blanket or not. God is even with us when we don't understand certain events. To prove her point she then told me the actual final story of the night, but it was one I'd heard before, well sort of.

By then her voice was a little raspy from staying up so late but she still went on with the story of the mustard seed. She said even the brokenhearted, confused, lost, or lonely all have at least a mustard seed of faith whether they realize it or not. She adjusted her version a bit, but I knew what she was talking about. She went on further by adding, the troubled, desperate, angry, or hurt have at least one grain. Sometimes they hide it, some deny it, and many never use it themselves but it's still there, and to prove her seriousness on the subject she called me by my first name and said, "Presley with that tiny mustard seed anything is possible, goodnight". She dropped the proverbial microphone after that beautiful story and we both fell asleep.

HOGWASH

The next morning came, which was only a few hours from when we went to sleep. Luckily most of the water around the restaurant had receded. Mamma Grace's biggest worry then was Diamond Lil's Cadillac but that flashy lady didn't care, she had another, and besides I'm sure it was covered by insurance anyway. I took Mamma Grace to Diamond Lil's house so she could get some real sleep and returned to the restaurant. I wasn't back any longer than 10 minutes when people started trying to come in to get an early breakfast. I simply wasn't ready. I opened the door for them anyway and asked everyone to bear with me, most understood, but Greg was a little huffy. I did have a little more compassion towards him after I heard about his past, but he was still being an ass. There were times during the war when we had to stay up for days at a time, mostly because we were getting shot at, but I don't think I was ever as tired as I was the day after the Great Gaston.

I got everything up and running and since Mamma Grace wasn't there it didn't run as smoothly as normal, but we still got the job done. Thankfully that was one of the rare days that we weren't overly busy. I guess everyone was still trying to make up for a lost day. Many people in the area still didn't have power for a few days after but our lights came on before I got back from delivering Mamma Grace. I was still wishing they hadn't though. Not too long before closing on the day after the storm, a man in a nice shiny silver suit and slicked-back hair walked it. The color of his suit wasn't too far off from Diamond Lil's flooded car, but he sat down on one of those sparkly stools and started talking to one of the waitresses.

Instead of placing an order, I thought I heard my name called out and then I saw the waitress point at me. I thought to myself, *oh no not the tax man coming after me too,* but that wasn't it at all. He then came behind the counter on his own, which really wasn't allowed according to the health department, and held his hand out to shake mine. I wiped off my hands on a nearby rag and returned his gesture. He then took a stack of papers out of a manilla envelope and proceeded to tell me that he received my Forever and Always manuscript and wanted to tell me his plan. I then thought, *oh hell no, not another plan.*

This man proceeded to tell me that he was from Board & Board Publishing and they wanted to market my book throughout their overseas divisions to see how it did. It would go all throughout Europe, South America, and Australia. He said they'd have it translated at no cost to me. I thought to myself, well, that was mighty nice of him considering I never sent the thing in the first place, and I wasn't paying anything anyhow. At that point, without question, or a word from her about what she'd done, I knew one of Mamma Grace's plans got me too.

I must admit I couldn't be mad at her or her hidden agenda because it was somewhat exciting until the man said I wouldn't get any residuals unless it did well, but if it did, he'd release at least 100,000 copies or more in the United States. If they sold that would be quite a payday. While he was there, he pulled out a large sketch pad and some colored pencils. I'd never seen colored pencils like he had, they must have been some professional style, but it was wonderful seeing what they helped him create. He started drawing and coloring until before long he had what he and I both thought was the absolute perfect idea for a cover. He said that he had to send it to his art department to be finalized but that was his vision of what he thought it should be. I let him know that my one requirement was he had to put the words "Thank you" where the author's name usually goes instead of my name. He assured me that a lot of writers publish their work incognito so that wasn't going to be an issue. I knew I had to pay homage to the whispering real author.

That well-dressed man didn't seem to have a problem with my request, and in no time, he had his idea for my cover touched up even more. What he came up with was simple yet so complex at the same time. For a minute I thought that he had colored an analogy of my life, and in a way he did. It looked so perfect to me that I wondered if he received some of those whispers as well, or if he really was that good at his job. When he finished, he pulled out a contract. He must know Mamma Grace too I thought, with that old bait-and-switch move, but I signed it without hardly reading a word. I remembered enlisting in the military and that man's contract couldn't be any more controlling than that one was. I couldn't wait until the next day to tell Mamma Grace how her secret plan turned out, so I called her at Diamond Lil's house. All she did after I told her what had transpired was giggle again and remind me of her mustard seed story from the night before.

Many of us might not think we have enough faith at times, but that little lady sure did have enough for everyone. For some reason, I didn't feel as tired as I once was. I stayed up almost all of that night too imagining I was on an elaborate book tour traveling all throughout wherever that man said my book was going. Before I finally settled down to get some sleep that I'm sure I needed, Mamma Grace's stories from the night before reentered my mind. Again, I didn't want to feel too blessed because I was still a little scared, but I also felt I needed to find a way to help Mamma Grace help the others. She did so much for so many people her whole life. I just wanted to find a way to do something very special for her also. I don't know if I expected to turn into Charles Dickens or Mark Twain overnight after that original visit but that didn't happen. I didn't hear a word back from that slick-haired man or the publishing company for what seemed like forever.

When I did hear back the publishers told me everything was going fine. I didn't know what their definition of fine meant but to me, it kind of looked like a dud. Don't get me wrong, I was still grateful that I received such a beautiful gift but I also began to allow myself to dream about what could be again and that left me feeling a little vulnerable. When Mamma Grace wanted to do something, she may have called it a plan, but I don't know how much planning she actually did. It was more like inspired and almost immediate action. With her, there was no real hesitation or lack of faith. I'm not saying that everything she did worked out as she thought it would but her intended target was always left in a better place than before.

During the first week back after the storm I told Mamma Grace that I wanted to help her with whatever it was she was planning. She smiled and said that's why we were stuck in the restaurant all night and giggled again. That crazy lady sounded like she actually thought she controlled the weather. Joking or not, she'd been secretly plotting her steps long before she let me in on the secret. I can honestly say that once I found out what she was planning I would never come close to thinking about anything like what she came up with. As ridiculous as it sounds, and it was ridiculous, Mamma Grace said she was going to pretend like she was sick. She knew all of those friends of hers loved and respected her and maybe that would create enough motivation to get them to finally do what she wished for them. My first thoughts were if she remembered where she got that mustard seed story from because even I knew there weren't any verses on faking an illness through a fib to get someone to do better.

She didn't care though, just like my grandfather, she would do anything to take care of the ones she loved. She wanted to go back to Italy for a little while anyway to see her family. I think she said she had a wedding of one of her nephews to attend also but she just missed home. Her missing home was understandable, but I still thought this plan of hers was absolutely ridiculous. I said I'd help, and I did but this was almost over the line. For the month before she left, I have to give her credit, she tried hard not to have to deploy such a scheme. She spoke with her friends more often but they'd leave with their heads down more often too. I could tell her warning shots weren't working. They all must have had a glutton for punishment because they all kept coming in even more often.

That part I knew for sure came from my grandmother. Once I realized her intended action went past the point of no return, I followed her directions exactly as she asked. She was going to have me call everyone in the restaurant all at once. I don't think those people had ever been there at the same time, not even on Thanksgiving or Christmas Eve, but I did know if it was a request from Mamma Grace they'd do it without question. Then she was going to have me hand out a handwritten letter to each of them, of course from her. She said inside would be a little note of encouragement and a few carefully chosen tasks for each to accomplish while she was sick, ha-ha, I mean fake sick. This lady was nuts I thought but I still promised her, so I was hell-bent on doing exactly what she asked.

To me, this was almost like feeling too blessed and if she wasn't careful, she was going to wish a real sickness on herself. When I tried to bring those thoughts up to her, she replied, "HOGWASH". I then thought to myself old people and their sayings, but I was the one spouting out hogwash huh? It didn't matter once she got the ball rolling on her preposterous plan neither she nor I could turn back. Mamma Grace put all of her proverbial balls in that basket and dragged mine in there with her. I knew this one would be a hard thing to explain if it didn't work out but again Mamma Grace had that unmovable and unwavering mustard seed.

She planned to call that meeting of the minds on the Saturday morning after she left for Italy. I'd have plenty of help at the restaurant then so I would have the time to sit at the table with the others and deliver Mamma Grace's penance. I still can't believe I am going to do it but I am. On the day of deliverance, spinning that Rolex, Greg of course came in first, probably to get what he thought was the best seat or at least the most appropriate for him. Then Erick and Mary entered fussing about something. Then there was the mighty mouth, Paul. A few minutes later Scott came in with more duct tape than ever. Then George, looking for liver. Then Wyatt grimaced his way in shortly. Luke came in late and last and sat down. Diamond Lil wasn't invited. I later learned in some ways she was a special beneficiary of a few of Mamma Grace's intentions just without the assigned activities.

M. A. COLE

LYING TIME

Before I joined the group, I had the tables pushed together so everyone could sit across from one another. I was going for that King Arthur and his knights of the round table look but considering all of those guys were in their sixties it was probably more like Presley's hair club for older men's convention. Before they got there, I did get to reflect a little bit about the whirlwind that just left for Italy and the restaurant itself since I had it. In many ways that place was magical too. We've had every kind of celebration there. We've had weddings, funerals, birthdays, and every other kind of gathering known to man. I remembered that my first real responsibility there was peeling potatoes. I still had to stay in that imaginary jail but my grandmother would stack a few milk crates together as both my seat and work table. My grandfather would give me a paring knife and place a 50-pound sack of potatoes next to me. He'd then chuckle or smile and say get to work.

The first time he did all of those things that big loving jerk didn't even show me how to do what he wanted me to do. He wanted me to figure it out for myself. It wasn't rocket science but I was just a small kid and I'd never peeled potatoes before. Both my grandparents would check on me from time to time. They'd give me a little encouragement and sometimes lovingly adjust my attempts at peeling all those stupid potatoes. If I got too far off track my grandmother would tell me to get my *culo* moving and giggle or smile.

Thinking back, one of the funniest times I can remember was when some of White Lightning's hometown friends visited. Those country people were funny as hell. Other than repeatedly calling my grandfather by his nickname they literally argued about barbecue the whole time they were there. It wasn't just about the barbecue itself either. It was about whose butt was this or whose butt was that. I was a kid, and I thought it was funny any time I heard the word butt. I didn't realize until that day that the portion of the pig that we and many other people use to make such cuisine is named Boston Butt. Once I did, I laughed at that too. Those old moonshiners looked like they were going to get into a fight over who had the tastiest butt. I can remember thinking I was going to bust a gut listening to those men squabble that day.

I'd still laugh today if I ever heard anyone arguing over whose butt was bigger or who had the moistest butt. That is one thing I have to say about Helene's, I'll always be a child there to some degree in my mind. But that's okay. Even with all of Mamma Grace's friends I'll always give them some degree of respect. I was there to serve and that part of the restaurant life is special. For me, it was a learned humbleness that has nothing to do with position or age. It was more about putting the needs of others in front of your own. My family may have done that with something as simple as food, and my grandparents mastered that craft, but they taught it even better. Looking back, I realized I wouldn't be here if things had gone differently with Isa, if we both hadn't gotten lost. Even now, I'd trade everything in a heartbeat for her. But truthfully, things aren't so bad there for me either. Mamma Grace may have been serving out letters instead of juicy butts, but I could only imagine what will be stirred up after that meal is served.

I have to say when that day came, I was nervous for several reasons. The first was her plan was still so ridiculous, and the second reason was because one of those damn letters that she wanted everyone to read aloud in front of the others had my damn name on it. I waited until everyone finished eating and I went over and pulled up a chair at the end of the table. They all knew I was there to pass on a message about Mamma Grace, which basically meant lying to them about her fake illness. Either way, I gingerly passed out each envelope and asked them not to open it until I explained what was going on. Greg side-eyed me as he did Wyatt at times, but I didn't look up enough to see if anyone else was. I then took a few breaths and a little more time to think.

I knew that no one other than me and Elizabeth knew that Mamma Grace was back in Italy. Everyone else believed she just took a few days off at that point. I did know that I wasn't very good at lying because once you tell a lie, then you usually have to tell another, and before long, you're the one who's confused. As I was trying to delay my dastardly duties, I heard an ambulance's siren outside, and it reminded me that I needed to get to fibbing. It was like Mamma Grace even had the paramedics working for her and that was my signal to start. No matter how it went I already decided that I was going to read my letter last if I went at all. But I did start explaining with my own twist. I told the group that Mamma Grace asked me to tell all of them that she was quite sick and wouldn't be around for a while. She did, however, leave a letter for everyone that she asked to be read aloud in the order she requested. I made that last part up because I didn't want to hear all those old guys fussing about what order they were going to go in but I kind of told the truth about the first part.

They were all understandably shocked hearing the news about Mamma Grace being sick and asked me if I knew what was wrong. I told them that I didn't know but as soon as I did, I'd pass that news along. I should have told them the truth and said she's crazy for making me do something like this, but I didn't. Since Greg got there first, I decided he should read his letter first. I settled on the order of their arrivals being the same sequence of their readings. I really do think all of us would have done anything for Mamma Grace and this little ask seemed like no big deal at first. When Greg opened his letter, he started reading it to himself. I didn't have to say a word about him not following the directions because everyone else did. He shook his head and smirked. I'm sure he hadn't been spoken to in that manner in a long time, but it did cause him to comply.

Mamma Grace didn't just write heart-felt letters. She was so serious about her wishes and wanted each one of us to feel her words. It was more like a call to duty because she felt "time" was running out. In her eyes none of us were living the lives she felt we were meant to have, and she knew to truly get us to listen to her she'd have to more or less stab us in the heart. She didn't just stab us with a mustard seed either, she tore us up with that pen and paper. I'd never heard Mamma Grace be anything other than kind and supportive but this time she wasn't playing. She wanted true and permanent change and those specific orders were extremely clear in every letter. She wasn't doing it for herself. In truth, sick or not her final years were probably going to be spent in Italy anyway with her own family however she did want those that she loved the most from her past, and even me from her present to be who she believed God wanted us to be.

Although her plan made absolutely no sense to me from the beginning, I began to understand why her methods had to be so severe. None of us would have followed her directions without that pain. That's a pain that only the loss of someone you truly love causes. It's a different hurt and Mamma Grace knew it firsthand. She made sure everyone's letter was specifically directed at each person, however, she did start and end them all the same. At the beginning of each for a salutation, she included the Bible verse from Psalms 90:10, where it reads, "The years of our lives are seventy, or even eighty; but they are soon gone, and we fly away". I think she put that verse at the beginning of each letter to say hey wake up idiots, the shift is almost over, and we better get our *culos* to work. I was still more than half of everyone's age, but her message still strongly resonated with me, as I'm sure it was intended to do.

I knew what she said her beliefs about death were, when you have to leave your doing so to do much greater things in a much greater place, but she also knew a good life geared towards helping others here was one of the greatest blessings that anyone could have. That's what she wanted for all her friends. As Greg started reading his letter aloud Mamma Grace's opening lines about the 70 or 80 years must have taken hold. He read as if he was a child again wondering where all the time went and how he aged so quickly. My grandfather always said you can tell how much older you're getting by how fast Christmas' come back around. From the look on Greg's face, I saw that he felt he had a Christmas every month and soon it would be every week.

Mamma Grace's intentions for us were all on different levels, some were larger than others. Some were almost simple, while a few were damn near unimaginable, but I'm sure she painstakingly chose what she felt her heavenly whispers told her we needed the most. For Greg, she asked him to start teaching young men and women his trade. When he found those with the heart, he started out to help them get a good job or start their own companies. Mamma Grace didn't just ask us to do certain things, she fully laid the path for our success and for Greg she had already talked to the job agency in the area that mostly served the underprivileged. They saw Greg as a folk hero with all of his success and couldn't think of a better role model. Mamma Grace had their first meeting set up the next week for them to discuss the details. Then, as she did in every letter signed Love, Mamma Grace.

That whole group was the same age, but they still called our girl Mamma Grace. Mamma in Italian isn't just another word for mother, mama, or mom. It's a way to describe the most loving caretaker who just happens to be in charge most of the time. I can't think of a name that suited that woman any better, and I know that group could either. I'm pretty sure it didn't happen, but I can envision those guys calling her Mamma Grace when she was there with them in their youth throwing snowballs or pushing bullies away. Even when she was tutoring the stubborn, or consoling one of them after a loss, maybe even when she went to church with some. Strangely enough, after learning all I did about everyone it was as if I was always with them too. So understandably I know for a fact that Grazia Isabella Russo was always meant to be Mamma Grace. And now that beautiful soul wants all of us to be who we were born to be as well.

Greg was a smart guy, and his request from Mamma Grace was right up his alley, but he did ask the perfect question after reading his letter. Greg asked, "What does all of this have to do with Mamma Grace being sick?" To be honest I kind of figured something like that would be asked but I still wasn't prepared. Without thinking and making a ridiculous situation worse I said because she doesn't think she'll be here much longer, and she wants us all to change for the better before she's gone. What the hell was I thinking? I just made an illness into a probable death without even trying. I told you once you tell lie, then you usually have to tell another, and before long, you're the one who's confused, and there I was confused as hell. Everyone looked at me like I knew more than I did, but I assured them I didn't, and after that slip up I really didn't.

Once they settled down from, yet another shock Erick and Mary went next. They may have had the biggest ask of the day, but at least they didn't have any questions after their reading. If they would have, I may have said something else stupid like Mamma Grace had leprosy. Anyway, Mamma Grace set up a meeting with social services for them to consider foster parenting two specific children, a brother and sister who had been in the system way too long and sounded like had a life that was very similar to theirs. Like I said this was a big ask. Erick and Mary were older, and even if it was only going to be for a few years until the children went off on their own as young adults, Erick and Mary would be more like grandparents rather than parents. I knew that part would be okay based on my life, but I guess after thinking this may be Mamma Grace's final wish for them, they didn't seem to have a problem with it, at least not originally. Then as always, our Mamma signed Love, Mamma Grace.

I thought to myself I hope she doesn't ask me to donate a kidney or find the cure for cancer when it was my turn because that one was a pretty darn big request. I think Paul was a little nervous after hearing what Erick and Mary had to read, and rightfully so. Either way, he was next and shook a little as he tore open his envelope. Paul was already retired and had too much time on his hands looking for his next ex-wife so I couldn't imagine what Mamma Grace wanted him to do, but soon we all found out. Paul too ended up as a pretty smart man. I guess all that tutoring paid off, but Mamma Grace volunteered Paul once a week to teach a personal finance class at that same job agency where Greg was asked to help.

What scared me the most about Paul's expected duties was most of those classes were filled with struggling young single mothers. I thought to myself she may have just placed the wolf in the hen house, but I never said anything. Once again, Paul didn't say much after his reading either. Paul had a degree in finance and used to be a bigwig at an insurance company at one point in his life, so he knew he was more than qualified. Who he'd be teaching kind of scared me, but either way and once again, the letter ended with Love, Mamma Grace.

When it was Scott's turn, he not only had a letter but also a huge box. One that I didn't know was wrapped and hidden in the restaurant's supply room until after he opened his envelope. Even though it was probably a little embarrassing, inside that box were seven brand-new outfits with underwear and socks included. Mamma Grace also went down to the civil air patrol and enrolled him in one of the aeronautic courses. If he did well enough, he'd eventually be able to teach using what he learned, and what he already knew about aviation to others. She just knew he could benefit from getting out to other places and eventually contributing to others again. She left directions for him to stay well-groomed and that she never wanted to hear of him using duct tape on anything again. Then of course signed his letter, Love, Mamma Grace.

Scott was the most excited about what Mamma Grace wanted him to do. I think he wanted to get up right then, take a bath, change his clothes, throw my grandfather's watch on, and head over to see what Mamma Grace had set up for him. But he at least waited until we were all finished opening our letters. George's request was a little funnier than the rest and would have been easier for most of us, but not necessarily for him. Mamma Grace wrote how she visited all the little pubs and bars around and got George banned for life. I could visualize this little Italian woman arriving with a few "wise guys" threatening the owners about swimming with the fishes if they ever let George in again. She also bought him a year's membership at a gym and paid for a personal trainer for that time too. She even had a rough idea for a diet scribbled out on the back side of his letter. Then ended it by singing Love, Mamma Grace.

Wyatt never said too much anyway but even more than the others I think if Mamma Grace asked him to tear down a building, he'd tear down two. So, when it came to his request, not only was it fitting it was also somewhat welcomed. Not as much as Scott's with the visual excitement but more of a knowing that he wasn't going to be the one to let Mamma Grace down. Mamma Grace signed Wyatt up to help lead a division of the prison ministry at the same prison he had been in for so many years. He was going to be assigned to those who felt they were unfairly incarcerated. He was to go there twice a month and not only talk about his life, but also what they could do to help theirs while inside. Wyatt knew what kind of help Mamma Grace was talking about. It started with that book he'd often see her with when they spoke. Once again, his letter also ended Love, Mamma Grace.

Mamma Grace knew that there wasn't any little or big project that would instantly reunite Luke and Elizabeth. She did, however, believe if Luke asked, regardless of the years or the pain, Elizabeth would have said yes in a minute based on their talks. She still loved him and always would because he was the father of their two daughters, but either way that wasn't the goal. Mamma Grace knew that the Veterans Association had specific programs for cases like theirs. Her goal, which Elizabeth was fully on board with was to talk to the counselors together once a week just so each could get back in the other's life to some degree. Even though their two daughters were my parents' age Elizabeth knew she could get them there too. Mamma Grace wanted them to start mending the fences to hopefully become a whole family once again before it was too late no matter how it was structured. Then as always, she signed Love, Mamma Grace.

Luke didn't really respond that day, but I felt he was going to at least give it a try. Then there was me, jokingly before I started reading, I thought this wench better not blow me up too, but she did. She told me, no ordered me, to stop judging others. She reminded me that none of us fully knew another's story or the root cause of their behaviors. She also told me how proud she was of me in regard to the restaurant and the book among other things. I was a little embarrassed myself because everyone at that table had to know a lot of my judgment was often placed in their direction. If it would have stopped there I would have been fine, but of course it didn't, not with Mamma Grace.

She asked me to start looking for a buyer for the restaurant, and that she had a realtor coming to visit soon. She wrote about how selling it was one of my grandfather's, her surrogate father's, last wishes and one that he specifically sent her there to help enforce after he was gone. She told me of the freedom I could have with my gifts. When she said gifts, I almost went around looking for another big box and I would have much rather had clothes than what I was hearing but I knew what she meant. I knew she meant well too, and I also knew I was still young, in my twenties but I still didn't want to hear any talk about selling the restaurant. All the people I was sitting with looked around as if I was planning to close Helene's for good that day. The majority scrunched their eyebrows down. I guess to show they'd never let that happen. Either way, I didn't respond except to read her final words which again were, Love Mamma Grace.

And there you have it, our fake sick, possibly dying, little Mamma Grace's final letters were distributed and read aloud as ordered. As everyone got up to leave, some got up lighter and some quite a bit heavier. I was somewhere in between. I felt to a degree Mamma Grace betrayed me a little. She'd been helping me for months. That restaurant was going great so why the push? Also, all those people knew they were the ones that I judged the most, so her having me call myself out in front of them was uncomfortable too. Once I got over my feelings, I called Mamma Grace with an update as she asked. Even calling her was crazy because I had to push twelve or thirteen doggone numbers to get her phone to start ringing. At least the Italians have phones in their houses now, I thought.

I was still a little in my feelings when she answered. Right away she asked how everything went and right away I answered ridiculous. I told her how I accidentally took her unknown illness and elevated that bologna to a possible visit from the grim reaper. She laughed and said good I might need to use that later. It wasn't good, I thought, I felt like a double agent lost undercover in a case that may be doomed from the start. I had much more clarity about what she was trying to accomplish than before however, I don't think Einstein could fully figure this one out. She didn't talk long after I told her everyone seemed to be on board. She asked me to call her every couple of days to give her updates and that was it. She told me she loved me and believed in me and hung up. I sat there with the phone in my hand with no one else on the other end for another minute fully realizing once again that I've been Mamma Graced.

I was never mad at Mamma Grace I just didn't understand the need to change something that seemed to be working as well as the restaurant was. I did, however, feel that I could try and stop judging people starting with her friends and that would possibly be my version of baby steps. Over the next month, everyone including Luke and Elizabeth seemed to be at least attempting to follow Mamma Grace's desires. Scott was definitely the happiest and most on track. The civil air patrol realized he knew as much as they did so they gave him instructor status within a few weeks. He was on cloud nine and always came in looking quite dapper. He even started eating a much wider variety of food too. Maybe there was a method to her madness after all, at least with Scott, I thought.

Both Greg and Paul began teaching at the job center and both seemed to be really helping and enjoying themselves. Often, they'd come into the restaurant together and that never happened before. I haven't even seen Greg spin his Rolex around once or heard Paul say anything inappropriate about the young women in his class. Even better Erick and Mary were approved to have a fourteen-year-old boy named Ben and his fifteen-year-old sister, Jessica come stay with them until they graduated or longer if they wished. Heck, even old George looks a lot more bright-eyed and bushy tailed, He's probably lost about twenty pounds and by the look in his eyes, I don't think he's had a drink either, not that he'd want to take a chance of being the cause of anyone having to swim with the fishes.

Everyone knew that Wyatt would follow Mamma Grace's directions but instead of doing what she asked, he goes to the prison even more and helps out everywhere he can. Me on the other hand I'll say I'm still fifty-fifty because I did run the real estate agent out of the restaurant but I'm not judging myself or others for it. I talked on the phone with Mamma Grace about twice a week as she asked after that original report and I still have to push all of those damn numbers to get to her. She was enjoying being back home with her family as she should. I was happy for her and still grateful she loved us so much to be making us do all of these things but I still had no intention of selling my grandfather's restaurant.

M. A. COLE

BILL BOARDS

I felt so guilty as the weeks went by because one week, I had to tell everyone Mamma Grace was getting better and the next not so much. I still never said what ailment she had because I knew thankfully she didn't have any, besides, no one really pushed on that topic thank goodness. Every time someone asked about her, I couldn't remember what I told the last person anyway. It was like this never-ending Ferris wheel and remember I don't like heights. I told Mamma Grace I didn't like doing what she was making me do, but she'd always change the subject and hurry off the phone after.

Even though I don't want to admit it I did know why the guilt about this situation was bothering probably more than it should have. Before my grandmother died I had guilt like this but even worse. Don't get me wrong, I loved my grandmother as much as my lungs needed air but once I realized she wouldn't be with us much longer I was almost mad at her for having to go. I know it was selfish of me, and I knew I really wasn't mad. I was just broken from knowing our family would never be the same without our guiding light. That was a hurt like nothing I'd ever felt before. It wasn't long after that those feelings were more than multiplied with my grandfather. I don't know what those two heartbreaks times infinity equals but it was worse.

Other than spending almost all of their lives in that restaurant, my grandparents had as good of a life as any. I definitely know they are in a much greater place, but I can't see them doing any greater things than what they did with their family. That is the part I get stuck on. I understand people can't live forever. We simply weren't created that way, but I almost wish there would be some way for us to be able to come in together and go out together as well. This is one of the many areas that Mamma Grace and I differ. Instead of feeling guilty about what she can't change or control she's doing all she can towards what she believes she can. That is also why I'll help her forever and always regardless of how ridiculous the plan may be.

Miss Grace still frustrated me a bit when she'd rush me off the phone if she didn't hear what she wanted to but for all I knew she was doing some Italian lady stuff that I didn't need to know about anyway. Besides, I knew she was trying to get back to somewhat of a regular life herself after her husband's passing. Knowing that she's multicultural once again she's probably making a bunch of plans for other people over there too. As another week went by that same man who told me my book, Forever and Always was doing fine came back into the restaurant but this time he brought company. He brought another man who wore an even nicer suit in with him. I almost thought I saw that new man spinning a Rolex around too but that could have just been my imagination.

He once again took it upon himself to walk back into the kitchen on his own to greet me, and I once again wiped my hands off on a nearby rag and shook his hand. He asked if I could come and sit with them for a while. I told him of course but I had to finish cleaning first. I think the man was a little shocked that I didn't drop everything right then and there and rush on over to see what they wanted but I've been haunted too many times by someone telling me that they were going to bust my *culo* if I didn't finish my work first. It didn't take too long for me to do as he asked and once seated with them, I shook the hand of his boss, who was also his father. I did like the family connection, so I relaxed a little to hear what they had to say.

I could never remember the first well-dressed man's name but once I met this new older guy, I don't think I'll ever forget either one again. I was meeting Bill Board Sr. and Bill Board Jr. again from Board & Board Publishing. In my sarcastic mind, for some reason, all I was thinking was. "there's your sign". Anyway, Mr. Board Sr. told me that my book was starting to sell in Europe and asked if I would consider going on a book tour. I thought that those two must have been in my room spying on me when I was imagining such, but he was serious. His explanation of what he wanted me to do was go around to various bookstores and libraries in certain cities throughout Europe, mostly in Germany, Italy, and Spain. It would still be at my expense of course but again I was told if the book did well, they'd also start selling it in the States. I was waiting for some other kind of bait and switch at that point, not that the at my own expense wasn't enough, but I did agree to think about it and get back with them.

It was a pretty good meeting I thought, at least I'm selling books that I never knew I would. I didn't realize I'd be asked to pay to try to get people to buy my book myself but the meeting overall wasn't bad. The difference between my version and theirs was, in mine somebody would be paying me. I wouldn't even be very particular about who that was either. As the men left, we shook hands again and I really did start wondering if what they had requested was normal, or if it really was a sign of some sort. I was a fish out of water with this publishing stuff and besides I didn't even send in the manuscript myself. I decided not to tell Mamma Grace about what happened mainly because nothing really did.

Those men just offered for me to pay for myself to go overseas and sit in a bunch of libraries or the like. I think after that day I settled on the thought that I couldn't leave the restaurant anyway. Besides it may not have been much but at least there I got paid. After putting that dream that I didn't know I had aside. It wasn't long before I started to notice something that wasn't going to sit very well with Mamma Grace. Except for Wyatt and Scott who were still superseding what was asked of them, all the others seemed to be falling off from their responsibilities regarding what Mamma Grace asked of them. Again, with this double agent thing, I was getting frustrated, but I didn't know what to do.

I knew none of those men were going to listen to me or even what I would say if they did. Erick and Mary did have the teenagers with them, and they all came in together quite often but all of them looked so overwhelmed. Paul said Greg was being too critical of the ones he was training, and Erick claimed Paul didn't show up for his class half the time. This plan of Mamma Grace's was turning into a train wreck. I have no idea what happened to Luke because he only comes in about once a week now and all he wants to know is how the others are doing with what Mamma Grace asked them to do. He barely spoke before but now all of a sudden, he's so nosey about the others and about me.

This whole plan has been a house made from straw and it looks like it's going to get blown down soon. I know with Mamma Grace not around I'm going to be the one that gets barbecued. Even George who was doing so well at first, looks as if he fell the fastest because Mamma Grace may have gone to all the bars and pubs nearby, but she evidently missed the liquor stores. I'm pretty sure he was three sheets in the wind the last time he was in, this is crazy I thought. Mamma Grace had the best intentions, God love her for that, but this powder keg is about to blow. I'm not excluded myself from this group of disappointments either. I'm sure she followed up with the real estate agent that I threw out and knowing her that may have been part of the reason she has been so short with me. I guess for all of us we've handled what she's asked us to do as an out of sight out of mind kind of thing because Mamma Grace herself hasn't been around to make sure we followed her directions.

I know she deserves so much better. I would think we all knew that. I waited another week to try to tell Mamma Grace what was going on, but I just couldn't. I pretended all was well mainly because I didn't want to be the one to break her heart. So, not only was I lying to the group, but now I was also lying to Mamma Grace and that was something I never thought I'd do. I told you once you tell a lie, then you usually have to tell another, and before long, you're the one who's confused. There I was once again, confused as hell. I knew I had to tell her I just didn't know how I was going to do it, or how she was going to take the news. I kept thinking about how I always told myself I'd help her forever and always. That wasn't just a pun on words or a sarcastic comparison to my book title that is what I thought I meant.

I am having trouble understanding how any of us could disappoint someone who has been there so much for all of us. That beautiful woman never gave up on any of us, especially her older friends. It seemed we couldn't even inconvenience ourselves enough to do a few things she asked. All her wishes for us were only meant to help our lives. Doesn't everyone understand that time is running out for all of us? Mamma Grace had been back home for less than six weeks and although it seemed longer I knew I had to do something drastic before all of the wheels fell off.

I decided to call another group meeting again without Mamma Grace knowing. The only way I knew I'd get everyone to attend was to say it was another request from Mamma Grace. I was unfortunately getting so good at lying that I didn't see how another lie could hurt but so much, but it did. My plan this time was to confront everyone and remind them what she had done for all of us to see if I could get everyone back on track before, I had to finally tell Mamma Grace the truth. Everyone agreed to meet at the restaurant that Saturday morning.

Like before I pushed the tables together so we could all sit together. I even rehearsed what I was going to say. I may have been discovered as a traitor in their eyes for threatening to tattle but I didn't care, I truly didn't know what else to do. This time in my life reminds me of the saying if you want God to laugh tell him your plans. Well, I don't think He laughed but I don't think He liked my plan either. When we all gathered that Saturday morning for our meeting regardless of how much I rehearsed or thought I knew what I was going to say I never got a chance to say a word.

M. A. COLE

NO WORDS

There are no words to describe what I felt that Saturday morning. At first, I thought it was just another one of her plans. Mamma Grace herself even joked about it when she said she may be able to use that later but this time as much as I wanted to believe that's what it was, it wasn't. We were all there except for Luke, no one ever saw him that much anymore anyway, but I thought he'd at least show up for another one of Mamma Grace's requests. I hummed and hawed around a little and made sure everyone had something to drink before we got started. Then finally, Luke decided to "Grace us" with his presence.

We all noticed something was wrong as soon as he came in. His eyes were bloodshot red as if he'd been crying all night. Remember this is one of those old leather-neck veterans who probably hasn't cried since he was a baby but this time it was obvious. Luke wouldn't even sit down with the rest of us. Instead, he put a single letter down in the middle of the table and then ran out of the restaurant. We were all looking at each other as to say what the hell just happened, but no one verbalized those obvious thoughts.

Not even Greg wanted to reach for that letter. It was almost as if someone put a rattlesnake in between us and no one would dare touch it. Seeing that no one else did, I finally reached for it and opened it myself. There were actually two letters in that one envelope. One from Mamma Grace and the other from Ana, her oldest daughter. I had no idea which one to read first but I had a gut-wrenching feeling that her daughter's letter may hurt a little less. I couldn't have been any more wrong. It had been over a week since I talked to Mamma Grace on the phone. I was doing the best I could to avoid her to see if I could fix our situation myself but I never got the chance.

Ana's letter wasn't long at all, but each sentence took what seemed like forever for me to get through. I felt I knew where it was headed even though I didn't want to believe it. Ana wrote about how much her mother, our Mamma Grace loved all of us, her friends, and how she cherished the past few months at Helene's. She wrote a bit about how she loved her mother too, and how now Mamma Grace has left us for a greater place to do greater things.

Again, a part of me thought this was just round two of Mamma Grace's ridiculous plan. Maybe somehow without me telling her she knew that most of us weren't doing anything close to what she asked. She may have just wanted to lovingly stab us all a little deeper to get us going for good. But hearing those words about how she was now in that greater place made me know what I feared the most was actually so. I'm sure those words are how Mamma Grace taught Ana to think about death. It was the same way she explained it to me. But God knows how I didn't want to hear them again.

Regardless of how rough and tough or even uncouth many of us have been along the way there wasn't a dry eye at the table. Now none of us will ever speak to, see, or hear Mamma Grace again. By now death and loss had been such a big part of my life, with my military friends, my grandparents, and even Isa came to mind. Losing that girl was always like a death to me too. With this news being so fresh the numbness that often comes with such a loss never came. This felt more like a prickly swelling in my heart that could explode at any time. I'm sure that was from the shame of letting such a beautiful soul down right before she had to leave. I knew I didn't want to read Mamma Grace's letter after reading Ana's. I didn't think I could get through it but somehow, I did.

Unlike the last individual letters, this group letter wasn't stern or directive. It wasn't full of plans or wishes for us either. It was simply one of the most soul-crushing apologies to everyone sitting at that table and to some who weren't. That lady's words tore us apart as she wrote about how she failed us and let us down. Her letter reminded me of when my grandfather said he had regrets. We knew Mamma Grace had absolutely nothing to apologize to us for. All she ever did was try to help, and she always went way above and beyond.

We knew she had it backwards, it was us who let her down, it was definitely the other way around, and we'll never get the chance to let her know. Shame and guilt doesn't come close to describing what I was feeling, and what I know the others felt too. A few of those who you would never think would, were openly sobbing. Paul and Greg were included in that mix. Older men don't usually cry like that but again most people don't lose someone like Mamma Grace. No one really wanted to talk after I finished reading both of those letters. I know for me all that needed to be said, was.

How I prayed it wasn't so. I tried to call Mamma Grace's phone after everyone left. I tried then and many more times after. I wanted to see if anyone would pick up, but there was never an answer. I felt I needed to find out what happened even though it was too late by then. Again, just like in my earlier life, everyone seemed to disappear. We never heard a single message about her funeral or anything else until about a month later and that was when I received a call from Ana. I didn't ask about the funeral because I figured if she didn't invite us, she didn't want us there but Ana did say that she knew we had an annual Thanksgiving event and she and her family would be in town and was wondering if they could come.

Of course, I told her I would love to meet them and that I was so sorry about Mamma Grace. Similar to her mother, when she heard all she needed to hear she rushed me off the phone and hung up. That was an unexpected, welcomed, and painful call all at once. I never thought things would come to this, but they have. The month or so preparing for that special day was always so much fun. Even though Mamma Grace's time there was brief, I couldn't see it being that much fun this year because we lost yet another big part of that place.

Again, for the life of me, I prayed that we could all be able to come in this life together and go out together as well, but I knew that was going to be just another unanswered prayer before I even prayed it. Mamma Grace was gone and so was another chunk of me. I knew I hadn't known her very long, but it was as if I knew her forever in no time. She was like Enzo, the husband she chose who had all the best qualities and traits of everyone she loved. That's what she was to me.

As odd as it sounds, right before I couldn't hurt anymore that faint whisper returned. This time it didn't want to give me a book title or tell me to let my grandfather's watch go. It didn't want anything other than to remind me. "The years of our lives are seventy, or even eighty, but they are soon gone, and we fly away". I'm not saying that definite whisper was Mamma Grace and I'm not saying it was God. I'm not saying it was anyone because I didn't know who or what it was, but I knew it was real, as real as anything I've ever heard.

That whisper, as slight as it was, probably, should have put more stress on my heart, but it didn't. Instead, it gave me at least a glimmer into the fact that there is another who is even a greater planner than Mamma Grace. Those plans may seem ridiculous and even incomprehensible at times, but still made by who loves us all the most.

Maybe a passage from my book, which was just a similar summation of other thoughts created from those whispers could say it the best, "When the heavenly stars say we can no longer be together, your heart and mine will still be intertwined always and forever". Mamma Grace and the others that I've loved and lost will always have my heart, and they always will because our hearts will always be intertwined. No time, or space, or even event, good, or bad could ever change that. For me, that last whisper was the confirmation that I needed but finally and fully understood.

M. A. COLE

REDEMPTION

L ife seems to last but a minute and Christmas' do speed up. Some get seventy, eighty or more years, while others get a few years or less. Either way, we all have a purpose, a reason for existing. Some find their purpose, some don't, and some are stuck bouncing back and forth between the light and the darkness. Either way, just like the mustard seed, our purpose is still there. For me, and the others who were so hurt by Mamma Grace's final envelope. The one that was filled with two equally painful letters, our acknowledged and redeclared purpose was to finally and fully fulfill the dreams of our angel. The angel who was here and is now above but still and always will be intertwined in our hearts.

Almost immediately Greg and Paul got on track. Paul still owned the company but retired from actually working to spend the majority of his life helping those achieve what he did and more. Paul never missed a class again nor was he ever anything other than respectful to everyone, especially those in need. Although it will take a little time to completely get there, George loves himself again, so he can accept love from others. Scott and Wyatt, well they found their purpose earlier and never looked back. Erick, Mary, and the kids are figuring it out one day at a time. They all found that little mustard seed inside of themselves.

Luke, Elizabeth, and their two daughters are taking baby steps, but it seems they were doing that long before Mamma Grace's letters. As for me, I'm thinking more and more about freedom every day. This time at least I didn't kick the real estate agent out of the restaurant. We are all so very far away from perfect but in dedication to someone who put us all on a very special personally chosen path we're going to get as close to perfection as we can.

Where there was once only pain from the loss of someone so very special there is now hope and loving memories. It didn't take long, it took real love and an understanding that she didn't have to be with us for us to feel her loving push once again. We were all somewhat sorry we didn't completely feel that push before, but again, I guess that wasn't in this particular plan. When I told the real estate I was going to sell I knew most likely that would be my last Thanksgiving at the restaurant and with coming so far so quickly we all should now be able to have a little fun getting ready for it, and for meeting the family of the one who caused all of this lasting change.

Mamma Grace so lovingly served others, but she may have taught it even better. From my grandparents with her in their early years, to her with me and everyone else more recently and back then, it has all come full circle, and what a beautiful realization that finally is. I'm sure from the first day my grandparents opened they started building a large family, both blood-related and many more not necessarily related by blood, but family just the same, kind of like we are now. Another thing I learned from Mamma Grace is sometimes you have to get out of your own way. A perfect example is as soon as I decided to let the restaurant go I received another sign, and once again that sign was from Bill Board Sr. and his son.

A week before Thanksgiving the pair came in. Still dressed very well if not better than before but it was almost as if they were play-fighting trying to see who would get in the door first. Either way, they were happy to be there and to ask me to come sit with them again. This time I didn't mind if the younger one came back in the kitchen on his own to see if I would. As we headed to the table his father didn't shake my hand this time. He ran up and hugged me instead. That man hugged me like he was the world's strongest gorilla.

I told you he was happy, but I didn't know why he felt he had to so forcefully violate my personal space like he did. I don't remember whether it was him or his son who told me after I could breathe again that we sold out of all the copies of Forever and Always in Europe. I thought he was probably talking about something like the 100 copies I gave away at the register, of course minus what Mamma Grace stole.

That wasn't it though. Actually, that wasn't anywhere close. He then pulled out a check that had as many zeroes after the 1, as I did barstools in that restaurant. Board and Board Publishing sold over 500,000 copies of Forever and Always and has another combined order for that many more for its overseas distribution alone and hadn't even started in the States except for the rights to a movie deal. This might be even better than the lottery I thought.

Almost immediately after the men left a ridiculous almost incomprehensible plan of my own entered my mind. Of course, that huge check would have to clear first but this time it wasn't whispered, it was chimed between my ears like one of those little monkey toys with the cymbals, relentlessly clanging until I understood its message. Once there was no doubt I wasn't dreaming, and I didn't have to worry about how I was going to fill my gas tank anymore. I asked some of the old gang to meet me at the restaurant.

George, Mary, & Erick specifically, and they all obliged. I didn't beat around the bush and I didn't say it was immediate but I did tell them that I wanted to give them a gift that was a huge part of my life. One that at times seemed like a family member itself. One that also seemed like a prison at times too, imaginary or not. It was a gift that had a six-foot, very life-like statue of Elvis Presley standing in the corner. For authenticity, it had a Gibson J-200 acoustic guitar proudly strapped across the king's right shoulder. That damn statue scared the hell out of me on more than one occasion when I'd sometimes have to open the restaurant way before daylight.

I had to make sure they fully understood there are days you just love the restaurant life and some you simply hate. There were many times I'd look at that kind of work as a self-chosen curse but if I was honest, it did bring just as many blessings, if not more. I chose those three as even partners because a restaurant can be a lot of damn work, but I couldn't imagine growing up in a better place. Other than those three being there the most, Geroge knows the most about food, no sarcasm intended, and he does so well with the kids and all our special events. As for Erick and Mary, they not only have two little potato peelers they also have a nephew who has always been more successful than me, and I'm sure having a professional golfer advertise for you would be great for business. Usually, I wouldn't recommend a partnership but I can once remember thinking I didn't necessarily need any help until this little Italian fireball times two busted in and just started washing dishes. I think she showed me and everyone around just how much we all needed her and we will forever and always.

Thanksgiving would be my final day there, my sunset if you will, but the next day unless there's another freakishly ridiculous storm will be George, Erick, and Mary's first day to make sure nothing else ever stops those doors from opening. They'll definitely see that the restaurant is more like a cranky old man than a fine wine. They'll have to fix things that break but overall if they keep serving that unique mix of mostly Italian and I guess you could say country food with gelato sprinkled with olive oil they'll all be blessed beyond their wildest dreams.

Greg and Paul were already more than okay so all I got them was just something they could spin around on their wrist. I don't think they will anymore but for me, that was the point. Scott has a new lawyer. That lawyer's suit and Rolex are even nicer than Bill Boards. He's going to see if that company can pay him for what was invented so many years ago with a little interest added of course. If for some reason that doesn't work, then we'll see that Scott gets enough to invent something even better. Wyatt & Luke didn't want anything for themselves, but the Veterans Administration and that prison ministry sure didn't mind taking a little money.

If Ben and Jessica ever feel ripped off by having to be at the restaurant so often as I had to in my youth possibly when it's time their new grandparents Erick and Mary can remind them, they never drove to school, or to work in cars like those two kids have. They had to walk to school uphill both ways. Finally, even though it probably won't arrive until after Thanksgiving, Mamma Grace's family is going to receive a little mail of their own. Those are addresses I didn't have any problem finding. One of the only things I asked, other than to make sure no one gets into an argument about a juicy butt, was to treat the restaurant as it has treated my family for all those years and if they didn't, don't be surprised if they get haunted by someone telling them that they were going to bust their *culos*.

TURKEY DAY

Someone said that Mamma Grace's family was staying with Elizabeth after they arrived in Richmond. You know how people are, they talk in little places like we have, or I had. Whoever it was, said Ana must have brought eleven or twelve of her relatives with her. They continued by saying, yeah you know those Italians; they like to have a good time. I was a little excited and scared all at once about meeting Mamma Grace's family the next day.

Considering all that has happened in such a short amount of time I began thinking about the word grace. I've heard to make sure you say grace before your dinner. I've also heard by grace, so and so have been saved. I've even heard that there was once a beautiful actress in the 40s named Grace Kelly who became the Princess of Monaco. I think she may have had more zeroes behind the 1 on her checks than I did but I'm not complaining. Maybe I'll make it to Monaco on a book tour someday. But grace from what I understand is based on divine intervention. It can make the impossible possible regardless of the recipient's actions.

Defined that way, there's no wonder why our beautiful, sassy, and stubborn Mamma was named Grace, but again I'm sure that was the plan. When the festivities started the next day, the place was as packed as I'd ever seen it, and as you know I've seen it a lot. I guess free food will make a restaurant that way. It wasn't just George that helped out this year either, it was the whole gang led by George, Erick, and Mary. All day people came and went but each seemed to be served to as close to perfection as we could get. We had the 50s music playing all day. If I tried just a little, I could see the silhouette of my grandmother shaking her little Italian booty over there next to the jukebox. If I squinted just a tad, I could also see the outline of my great big grandfather and his giant hands chopping up some of those moist butts.

I could go on all day about those butts because I still think that's funny, but seriously if the light hit just right, I thought I could even see a shadow of our little Mamma Grace putting olive oil on something you wouldn't think it should go on. That day the place seemed perfect, not just as close to perfect as we could get but perfectly perfect without question.

I guess because Ana had so many family members come over from Italy they had to take a few cars to get there. The first group to come in was Ana, her husband, and their kids, who again weren't kids because they were both around my age. She said the next crew was on its way and I'd be able to meet more of Mamma Grace's family then. The restaurant was so busy and so many people heard it was my last day that everybody seemed to want to talk to me. Many of those people were the ones who helped us stay open all of those years and were a part of that non-blood related, but related just the same family.

I felt like a chicken with my head cut off, running around talking to everyone. It was so hectic that I didn't notice Ana's second group of family members out of three come in. I guess they had 12 people total and there were 4 to a car, which makes sense if they had 3 cars. Anyway, I'm sure she understood that I'd go over and speak when I could, but we really were that busy. George had that doggone puffy white chef's hat on again playing with all the children. Ben and Jessica were doing better than I did at their age with helping out. Erick and Mary kept the food coming out all day. Most of the rest of the group, Wyatt, Scott, Paul, and Greg were on dish duty. I never thought I'd see Greg wash dishes but he washed as many as anyone.

What made me stop in my tracks was when Luke and Elizabeth and their two daughters came in and sat down together. That Mamma Grace is something else, I thought. Other than that brief stoppage I really couldn't pay attention to anything else, but for some reason, I kept having DeJa'Vu. You know that feeling of already experiencing something. That was more than understandable because in a restaurant many days feel the exact same with the same things occurring over and over again, but this was different.

I felt like I'd seen the scene before. I didn't just feel it, I would have sworn I lived it in some way before. Everybody else was so busy that they didn't have time to look around and see who was coming or going out, but I had to stop at least for a few minutes to see why this one particular table was collecting so many bottles of olive oil. I knew there were a lot of Italians in the restaurant at the time but regardless for some reason, I think that collection of bottles was triggering those feelings of familiarity.

When I arrived at the table I didn't think I saw a ghost I knew I did. The most beautiful, sassy, and stubborn little Italian Ghost lady that God ever created, and I wanted to choke her. It was that non-answering the phone, letter writing, thankfully alive lying wench Mamma Grace sitting right there with all of her family. Like I said before I always thought of myself as a big tough ex-military guy but when I saw her, I screamed out like a teenage girl, fell to the ground, and started sobbing.

Even Mamma Grace knew she had gone too far with that plan, but it was done, and no matter what she was still with us. Everyone else ran over when they saw me crying on the ground and after they saw her every one of them did the same. Our angel, that lying old pain in the butt, storytelling, loving lady was trying so hard to put her arms around all of us all at once.

We all cried together for what seemed like an hour except for Luke and Elizabeth. They never got up from their booth as if they were all a part of plan B, and that's because those idiots were. If I was a double agent that meant Luke was a double-double agent. He'd been feeding Mamma Grace the information that I was too afraid to tell her. They both knew I wasn't going to tell on myself so he was also telling her everything about me along the way too. Luke's letter was even a rouse from the beginning to set up a possible backup plan if needed.

He and Elizabeth, along with their daughters were going to the VA for family counseling for months before all of this craziness went down. That jerk even said he put soap in his eyes when he delivered Mamma Grace's final letter for effect but it burnt so bad he had to run out of the restaurant after. I thought to myself, jack ass, that's what you get. This day just became surreal but regardless Mamma Grace was with us all once again.

None of us could stay mad at her even though that ridiculous plan went way beyond too far. I know there weren't any more dishes washed for the rest of the day and everyone else that came in had to serve themselves because none of us would leave Mamma Grace's side. Part of that was we were all scared that she'd come up with another ridiculous plan.

That woman absolutely infuriated me, but all I could do was hug her and try to hold back my tears. I don't think anyone else knows someone who would go through so much trouble or have a double, and double-double agent to make sure her friends and family have the best life they can. The lives they were born to have regardless of the cost.

I still wanted to put her in time out or make her peel a whole fifty-pound bag of potatoes by herself though, but I just couldn't. I love her too much. I know she wanted us all to accomplish things in life before our time ran out, but she aged me at least twofold that day alone. This crazy woman is just too much I thought.

FOREVER AND ALWAYS

Once everything calmed down as much as it could, and we all got a little more used to Casper the conniving Mamma Grace ghost being back, Ana told me that most of her family had arrived except for her cousin, his wife, and their daughter. They had to take a later flight because her younger cousin, the daughter, had been fighting cancer for the last five or six years and she'd been in and out of the hospital near Palermo all of that time. The family had to move in with her other sister just to be able to afford to get the girl, who was also about my age, the treatment she needed. She'd been in full remission for a while, but this last doctor's appointment was the one that fully cleared her to go out and live her life again.

She thought they'd arrive shortly but made the comment that at least they'd have my book to read on the flight over. I didn't know what she was talking about at first but evidently, on some flights flying out of Europe, you had the choice of a movie or whatever book they had to offer. In this case, Board and Board Publishing must have made mine available for those flights coming out of Italy.

Ana told me how her whole family loved my book and how she left a message for her cousin to make sure they chose the book over the movie too. My name wasn't on the book, I just had *"Thank you"* where the author's name goes, but I still knew how she knew it was me who wrote it. Ana was so interested in the main character, which as you know was Isa. I think because she was an Italian woman, and I am an American man it must have seemed like one of those tele novellas that are so popular now.

I really wasn't aiming for a soap-operish book and that's definitely not what I got from the whispers, but I could see in a way what she was talking about. You know boy meets girl, boy loses girl, boy really-really loses girl, boy loses himself, boy finds himself, so on, and so on, sure it's all the fad, I guess.

Anyway, I told her regardless of the time I'd make sure on my last day of restaurant ownership we'd stay there as long as her family wanted. I was still side-eying Mamma Grace myself while we were talking because I didn't want that lady to cause any more trouble. I still think if she had ordered some of that olive oil gelato, I may have put ex-lax in it. I just can't believe she did what she did but even more, I can't believe she's back with us once again even more.

When her cousin and his family came in, me and the father kind of stopped and stared. It was as if we'd seen each other before. I thought it was possible because I was based in Italy, but other than that I just wasn't overly sure. That was about five or six years ago anyway and I have a little beard now. I'm also in let's say better barbecue shape than I was then. The man's daughter went into the bathroom to freshen up before she met the famous author according to him.

At that point, I knew they all read my book on the flight over too but once again with my five minutes of fame, I could only be sarcastic with myself and think, there's your sign again. As sad as it might sound on any big occasion, I'd always take Isa's grandmother's ring and put it in my pocket. Even years later I'd pretend like Isa, my "imaginary" wife was wherever with me too. I told you it was kind of pitiful, but I really loved that girl no matter if she was really-really lost.

I had a few minutes, so I went to the back supply room to kind of decompress. I thought, Mamma Grace better hope I didn't find any ex-lax or potatoes back there but while I was sitting on one of those old milk crates. The ones my grandmother used to stack together as both my seat and work table I pulled out that ring. Like I have so many times, I held it in my hand.

Don't get me wrong especially with that little Italian crazy woman back from the dead, this very unexpected book deal, and the way I was able to help Mamma Grace's friends, I should be ecstatic, and I am. I am about 90% ecstatic without question, but I don't think I'll ever be whole again without my Isa. I just knew she was the one from the moment I met her.

I also knew it wasn't the time to wallow in anything, so I got up and started to return to the others. Besides this, pretend famous author had to go mingle with all of the new people who just showed up. For some reason, I forgot to put Isa's grandmother's ring back in my pocket. Instead, I walked out to meet everyone with the ring still in my hand. Before I got to the new arrivals, the man I thought I recognized earlier started to introduce me to his daughter who was behind me.

This was the second time I was on the floor that day because before I got a chance to turn all the way around his daughter leaned over and whispered, *"Sempre E Per Sempre"*, in my ear. I knew right then as well as my lungs knew they needed air, that was my Isa. I didn't even turn all the way around, I wanted to make better use of my time, so I dropped straight to one knee and held out my hand with her grandmother's ring in it. I didn't think there was an expiration date on a parent's blessing, and I didn't care where she'd been or what she'd been doing. Hell, I didn't even look to see if there was already another ring on her finger, which thank God there wasn't. But right then I knew Isa and her family were the ones who moved from Aviano to Palermo so she could have treatment. She was the one who had been fully cleared to go out and live her life again. She was also the one who read my book about herself on the trip over.

I knew then more than ever that there was a much greater planner than even Mamma Grace. It was about that time that her parents also realized what was going on, and who I actually was. They came over to where we were with the same confusion, hugs, and tears that we all had with Mamma Grace earlier. Her father was the second person in my life to hug me like he was the world's strongest gorilla, and Isa's mother was the third.

Me, well I wasn't getting off that one knee until I got an answer. I had my mind made up that once I found the love of my life again, there was no way I was ever going to let her out of my sight, again. It was going to be us, together, forever, and always.

THANK YOU!

Dear Friends,

Thank you for choosing our inspirational products! We'd love for you to visit our website at www.inkwillpublications.com to check out our full range of offerings.

With Love,
M. A. Cole